JUDGMENT DAY

A NOVEL

G. MICHAEL HOPF

DEDICATION

TO SCARLETTE

"Justice and judgment lie often a world apart."

- Emmeline Pankhurst

PROLOGUE

MAY 17, 1865

INDEPENDENCE, MISSOURI

James peeked his head over the log and stared at the cabin in the distance. The anxiety of the pending assault felt like a jolt of electricity shooting through him. Soon he'd be called to do what he'd been wanting to do all his short-lived life, defend the South and its heritage against the Yankee invaders.

"Harris, get your damn head down!" Cecil Brangan barked, ensuring he kept his voice down. Cecil was the second-in-command of Kemp's Raiders, a guerrilla resistance that had formed recently after General Robert E. Lee's surrender, which ushered in the end of the Confederacy. Cecil could only be described as scraggly and ornery, with many giving him the nickname Badger. His lean face was covered with a thick beard, and his reputation for fighting was renowned. He and John Kemp had met years before during the onset of the war and stayed in Missouri causing havoc. With the war over, they saw no

1

need to stop.

James ducked down and sheepishly replied, "Sorry, I was merely—"

"You were acting a fool. We stay quiet and keep our damn noggins out of sight until nightfall; then we go in and kill those damn Yankees," Cecil growled as he shook his head.

"Yes, sir," James said, feeling embarrassed. Having just turned sixteen, he had left home to oppose the Northern occupation of Missouri. James looked disheveled wearing his father's clothes; not only were they old and tattered, but they were too big for his lean frame.

Kemp's Raiders were a ragtag group made up of mostly young men. The veterans had mostly abandoned the cause and gone home to tend to their farms and families. For these men though, the war wasn't over; they vowed to never surrender.

Franklin Ashe crawled over alongside James and nudged him. "Don't look so glum. Cecil's hard on everyone."

"I just feel foolish," James confessed.

"Oh, don't feel that way. Say, this is your first time, isn't it?" Franklin asked.

"It is," James replied.

"My name is Franklin Ashe, and if it makes you feel better, this is my third attack," he said, holding out his hand.

James took his hand and shook. "I'm James Harris of Platte City. Nice to meet you."

"Same here, James Harris of Platte City," Franklin said

with a toothy grin.

"Were you scared?" James asked, referring to Franklin's first engagement. He genuinely wanted to know and hoped Franklin's answer was yes.

"Almost shit my trousers," Franklin answered. "Hey, did they tell you that you'll be tossing the torches in first?"

"I will?" James asked, the look on his face showing his fear and concern.

"Yeah, it's your first time, so you get the honor," Franklin said.

"Did you?" James asked.

"I didn't toss torches, but they had me stop this Yankee convoy. You could say I was the bait; then they gave me the honor of shooting the first prisoner," Franklin confessed. "While I was a bit nervous, Lucille was happy."

"Who's Lucille? I haven't met anyone with that name," James said.

Franklin pulled out his Remington 1859 New Army pistol and gently rubbed it. "This is Lucille. My pa gave it to me. He said it's the best gun out, much better than those Colts you're carrying."

"Is it?" James asked. While he was familiar with shooting and knew his way around his twin 1861 Army Colts, he wasn't knowledgeable about all the different pistols and arms in circulation.

"It sure is," Franklin said.

Curious about something Franklin had said, James asked, "You said something about shooting prisoners. We don't take prisoners?"

"We're not regular army. Plus with Lee surrendering, we're setting our own rules of engagement now," Franklin said.

"Do you think I'll get to shoot someone?" James asked.

"I wouldn't wager against it; just be ready. I suggest you have those pistols cocked and ready after you toss the first torch through the window," Franklin said, nodding to James' Colts nestled in holsters on both sides of his hips.

"They're loaded and ready to shoot," James said confidently.

"You ever shoot anyone before?" Franklin asked.

"Never," James replied.

"Just hit them in the center of the chest or right here," Franklin said, pointing at his forehead.

"How does it feel?" James asked.

"What do you mean?"

"To kill someone?"

"Oh, I suppose it feels alright. Killing Yankees feels satisfying. Seeing that blue-bellied Yank beg for his life before I put a round ball in his head made it even more special," Franklin said, lifting his chest slightly.

"How many Yankees are holed up in this cabin?" James asked.

"I don't know. I leave those details to Cecil and Major Kemp," Franklin replied. "Say, did your pa fight for the Army of the Mississippi, or did he stay in Missouri?"

James lowered his head and said, "He fought alongside Johnston."

"I bet he's proud of you," Franklin said.

"My pa died at Shiloh," James confessed.

"Sorry, my condolences," Franklin said.

"Ma has been sad ever since. She didn't want me to leave, but I made her swear that upon my sixteenth birthday I could go out and avenge him," James said.

Franklin put his hand on James' knee and squeezed. "Your pa would be proud, I just know it. Soon you'll get your chance to extract a pound of flesh."

"I'm looking forward to it," James said, a smile stretching across his youthful face.

"I like you, James Harris of Platte City. I think we'll be friends," Franklin said happily.

The two exchanged casual conversation for the next hour, stopping when Cecil approached James.

"You ready, boy?" Cecil asked.

James knew what that meant. With the sun just below the horizon, it was time to attack. "Yes, sir."

"Good. Now you're going to take these two torches up to the house and toss them in through that front window. As soon as you do that, fall back to the well house and set up in a defensive position. Those Yankees will start pouring out the front door, and you'll be able to start shooting. Now, are both those pistols loaded and ready?"

"Yes, sir, they are," James replied.

"Good boy," Cecil said.

"What will you all be doing?" James asked.

"We'll be right here covering you, don't you worry," Cecil said, giving James a reassuring look. He turned to another man and said, "Light those torches."

When the flames on the torches came alive, James

watched as they danced in the gentle breeze. He then grew concerned that he'd be seen as he traveled the hundred yards to the cabin. "Sir, won't they see me coming?"

"Not if you head down this creek bed and come around the back side. Once there, you have half the distance to cover to the front window," Cecil said.

James looked past him and down the dry creek bed, which was getting harder to see as each minute passed.

"You going to be able to do this? Tell me now," Cecil said.

"He's got this, Cecil. He's here to avenge his pa," Franklin blurted out.

"Is that right?" Cecil asked.

"They killed him at Shiloh," James answered.

"Your pa died a hero for the Confederacy, God bless his soul. Now take these torches and continue the fight for your old man, boy," Cecil said.

John Kemp appeared suddenly. He was a tall and sturdy man, towering near six feet three inches with broad shoulders and trunk-like arms. "James, I trust you got this."

Showing his nervousness, James removed his hat and said, "Mr. Kemp, how ya do?"

Calmly, John said, "I'm fine, thank you. Now take those torches and do as Cecil said."

"Oh, I will, Mr. Kemp, don't you worry," James said.

"That's a good boy, now hurry on," John said.

John took the torches from one of his men and handed them to James. Taking them firmly in his grasp, he gave John a smile and nodded.

John patted him on the shoulder and said, "Go kill

some Yankees."

With a broad smile, James marched towards the dry creek bed. He carefully made his way across the rocks and uneven ground until he made it to the point where he needed to exit the tree line. He didn't hesitate. He exited the woods and ran as fast as he could without extinguishing the torches. Making it to the side of the cabin, he could feel a sense of pride fill him. He was close now to avenging his pa. With his back against the wall of the cabin, he slowly made his way around to the front window and paused. He looked out towards where he'd been hiding for the past few hours and prayed they were ready to cover him once he tossed the torches inside. Knowing he couldn't wait any longer, he spun around, but just before he tossed them, he spotted three small children, a boy around eight and two younger girls, inside the cabin sitting at a table. *What are they doing there?* he asked himself.

"Do it!" Cecil boomed from the woods.

Hearing Cecil, James brought his right arm back and readied to throw the first torch but again paused upon seeing the children. *This isn't right*, he thought.

"Damn it, boy, throw the torches!" Cecil barked from the darkness.

Frozen in fear, James ran the scenarios through his mind. If he tossed the torches, his initiation into the rebel resistance would be sealed, but if he didn't, he might as well turn his pistols on himself.

"Toss the damn torches!" Cecil bellowed.

Thoughts of his mother filled his thoughts. What would they do to her? Would she be branded a traitor?

Would the spirit of his father recoil at his treachery? Fearful that his inaction would affect his mother and his family standing in the area, he tossed the first torch through the window but not before the boy inside looked out and saw him. The two locked gazes. It seemed as if they stared at each other for hours though it was merely seconds. The first torch smashed through the window, hit the table, and set the clothes of the children on fire. Howls and screams came from inside the cabin. Now committed to his cause, James tossed the second torch in. This one skidded across the table, hit the floor and rolled over towards a cot. The flame tickled a sheet that hung down, catching it on fire.

Frantic, James turned and ran to the well house, drew his twin Army Colts, and cocked them.

The small cabin quickly turned into an inferno. The screams of terror and pain continued to come from inside. The door opened, but it wasn't a Yankee soldier who came out, it was a woman no older than twenty-five, followed by the boy. Both were on fire. They hit the ground and rolled in an attempt to snuff out the flames.

James raised his right hand and aimed at them, but couldn't find the courage to squeeze the trigger. These were civilians not soldiers. Where were the Yankee soldiers he was told were in there?

Another woman exited the cabin, she too on fire. In her arms was a small body. Was it one of the girls or another unseen child, maybe a baby?

"Fire!" Cecil ordered.

The tree line erupted with a volley of gunfire.

Bullets rained down on the women and children. The

woman carrying the child was struck in her chest and stomach, causing her to drop the child. She fell to her knees, cried out, and toppled over dead.

Another volley of gunfire came from the guerillas, followed by another in quick succession.

James watched the scene in front of him in horror. With the pistol in his right hand extended, he waited for any soldier to depart the inferno, but none did.

A minute later the roof of the cabin collapsed, leaving only the four walls standing.

Out of the darkness, Cecil emerged. He marched over to James and yelled, "What the hell, boy?"

Tears were streaming down James' face. He stood and said, "Those weren't Yankee soldiers, those were women and children!"

"Well, I was told there were Yankees in there," Cecil said, holstering his pistol.

"There weren't soldiers, just children. I killed children; I killed innocent people!" James howled in protest, tears flowing heavily from his swollen eyes.

"Boy, I guarantee you those weren't innocents but Yankee collaborators, and around here that's no different," Cecil said.

"You said we would be killing Yankee soldiers not women and children!" James howled.

"Boy, you're acting impetuous. If you can't handle this war, best you go home to your mama," Cecil mocked.

"I came here to kill Yankees, not kill children. That's what I was told the Yankees do. Is that what we do now too? Are we no different than the Yankees?"

Cecil's steely eyes squinted sharply. "Best you shut your mouth, boy."

"This is a lie, a damn lie. Why did you have me kill those people, huh?" James asked, suspecting the attack wasn't a mistake but for a reason.

Hearing the dustup, John came up behind Cecil and said, "I ordered this attack. Our intelligence told us these people provided aid and comfort to the Yankee army and that soldiers are often here."

"But they weren't tonight," James spat.

"Makes no difference in this war, young James. Those people are Yankees, and until we kill every one of them, our land will never be truly free," John countered.

Anger welled up inside James. Still holding the twin pistols, a strong temptation to shoot both John and Cecil came over him.

Seeing him clench the pistol grips tighter, John asked, "You okay, James?"

"No, I'm not. You had me murder women and children," James replied.

"How about you holster those pistols before you make a very bad decision," John warned in his usual calm demeanor.

James looked down at the pistols and his white-knuckled grip. He pushed the temptation to shoot the two men out of his mind and tossed the pistols on the ground. "I'm done."

"You're done?" Cecil laughed. "I thought you came to avenge your pa?"

"My pa wouldn't approve of a Southern man killing

innocent civilians, no, sir, he wouldn't," James said.

"The war has changed, son; you need to understand this," John said, hoping he could convince James and soothe his passions.

Pulling his pistol and cocking it, Cecil pointed it at James and said, "Let me kill him."

John lowered Cecil's arm and said, "No, let him go. He came here and has shown us he doesn't have the stomach for the fight. Let him live in his own guilt. Once we've thrown out the Yankee invader, he'll come back, begging to join our ranks, but he won't be welcome."

"I don't want any part of this," James spat. "And guilt I do have. I helped you murder innocent women and children."

The other raiders were slowly walking up to the bodies on the ground, laughter and hoots emanating from them.

James looked in their direction and scowled.

"C'mon, let me kill him," Cecil urged.

"His guilt will eat him alive," John said with a smile.

"I know that God wouldn't approve of this," James said, pointing towards the bodies of the women and children. "You will find his justice and wrath for what you've done one day."

"You burned the cabin down, James, we didn't," John reminded him.

The urge to pick up the pistols and shoot John again came over James, but he knew any movement towards that would only result in him being killed. "You will be judged one day by God."

"James, you seem so confident for such a young man

about there even being a heaven or hell. I can tell you after four years of fighting that if God does exist, he doesn't care about us," John said.

"You're despicable," James hissed.

"Damn it, John, you're not going to let him talk to you that way, are you?" Cecil asked.

"Best you go now," John said to James. He cocked his head towards Cecil and said, "Trust me, his reputation is ruined, his family's too. His actions tonight will haunt this young lad his entire life. I can smell the guilt oozing from his skin like the sweat on a hot summer day."

Cecil shook his head in disappointment.

Not able to stand next to the men any longer, James turned and walked away.

"You should have let me kill him," Cecil said as he uncocked his pistol and holstered it.

"Like I said, his guilt will eventually kill him," John said.

PLATTE CITY, MISSOURI

Evelyn Harris, James' mother, paced the kitchen, her right hand massaging her neck while she contemplated the news James had relayed to her.

"Ma, I'm sorry," James said emphatically.

She stopped and barked, her nostrils flared, "Do you have any idea what you've done? Do you?"

"Everything will be okay. It will all smooth over in time," James said in an attempt to soothe her worries and his.

"No, it won't, son; this damn war has stirred up many tensions. There are far too many people that will hear about what you did, not just killing those women and children but that you also betrayed those bastards John Kemp and Cecil Brangan; those men are heroes of sorts in these parts, and now you're against them. You might as well go wear a Yankee uniform."

"It won't be that bad, Ma, I promise," James said.

"You're not just a boy but a foolish one. You know nothing about life. All you have is what most boys your age have, narrow-minded folly based upon misplaced fantasies of glory or revenge. Your pa never would have wanted you to go do what you did, never," she blared.

"Not true, he fought for the Confederacy, under the great General Johnston," James countered.

"He fought for the regular army, not some outlaw gang who have not only terrorized the blue coats but also normal folk. You think they're good people who are looking out for you; they're not. Their only interest has turned to enriching themselves. Just two weeks ago they robbed a train, stole from everyone, including good Southern folk."

Hearing her complaints, ones she never expressed before, he lowered his head and began to sob. "I'm sorry, Ma, I've dishonored you, Pa's legacy, and our good family name."

She walked over to him and lifted his head. Looking deeply into his green eyes, she said, "You're a Harris and a man now. There won't be any crying anymore. Yes, you made a mistake, a big one, but you now must live with the consequences. This is an important lesson. You can't just act from emotion. You need to make choices and judgments from reason. Use your head not your heart."

"But my life is over," he cried.

She wiped his tears from his cheeks, cradled his face in between her hands, and softly said, "Not true, my darling son, your life has only just begun. I won't say it will be easy, but you still have choices, options."

"And what can those be? I'm a murderer, a killer," he whined.

"James, stop crying and look at me. I need you to hear what I have to say to you," she said.

He sniffled, wiped his nose, and said, "I'm listening."

"I need you to go into your room and pack a bag—"

"Pack a bag? Where am I going?" he asked, his face showing the shock he was feeling.

"Son, your life is over not only in Platte City but all of Missouri; however, you can have a full life if you travel west, go to the territories, go to California. There you can be whoever you choose to be, you can even give yourself a new name, but James Harris from Platte City is now a thing of the past," she said soberly.

"You want me to leave?"

"I don't want you to go, but you must. I love you too much to see you suffer or be hanged for what you did," she replied.

"What will I do out west?"

"Anything you want. You're smart and you'll make the right decisions if you use your head. Don't lead with your passions, don't be like your father, God love him; but you

Harris men have a knack for fighting. You must squash that, be a peaceful man; violence only leads to trouble."

"Come with me," James said.

"No, my life is here; your father is buried out back. When I die, I'll be laid to rest next to him. No, son, this is where our lives together come to an end. I can't tell you how sad I am to say that, but if you're to have any real life, you must go and go now," she said, her eyes welling up with tears.

"No, Ma, please come with me," James pleaded.

She lifted him from his chair and embraced him with her long arms. Petting his head, she said, "I love you, James, and I always will. Now hurry, go pack."

***

James hurried and packed all his worldly possessions, which easily fit into a large sack. He slung it over his shoulder and exited his room to find his mother standing with a small box in her hands. "Will you please reconsider?" he asked.

"I won't. This is my home; yours is out west now. Go find it," she said.

"I don't know what to say except I'm sorry," he said.

She touched his face tenderly and said, "Take what's in the box."

He opened the lid and found a roll of currency. "No, I can't take your money, Ma."

"I insist. You'll need it to survive until you get on your feet," she said.

"I won't take it. How will you survive?" he asked.

"With you gone, there's no one to care for the farm, so I'm going to sell it and move into town. The proceeds from the sale will give me plenty to live off of until I can figure out how to earn a wage," she said.

"You're selling the farm?"

"Yes, I don't have the urge to do it anymore, and this really was your father's dream, not mine," she confessed.

Saddened by the news, he lowered his head. The heavy weight of guilt was taking a toll. He'd not only ended the lives of others earlier tonight but had also shattered his own life and that of his mother. Tonight was nothing short of a catastrophe.

Handing the cash to him, she said, "Take it."

"I won't," he insisted.

A smile broke out on her face. "You're as stubborn as your father and as prideful as me. If you want take it as a gift, at least take it as a loan. Will that work?"

He thought for a moment then said, "I will accept those terms. The second I can repay you, I will."

"Good," she said.

He took the money, shoved it deep in his pocket, and said, "I love you, Ma."

Embracing him, she said, with tears rolling down her face, "I love you too, son. Now go, hurry."

He refused to let go of her.

She pried herself away and nudged him towards the door. "Go to the barn and take your horse. Ride until you reach Kansas City; take a train from there anywhere west."

He began to cry as well. "Okay."

She wiped his tears, kissed him once more on the cheek, and pushed him out the door and into the darkness of the night. "Take care of yourself, James, and always know that I love you."

He slowly walked to the barn, thinking of all the trouble he'd gotten himself into. As he climbed onto his horse, he pledged that never would he foolishly enter into anything without rational and reasoned thought, nor would he ever engage in violence. He was not going to be that man again. He trotted out from the barn, looked towards the house with hopes he'd see his mother, but she was gone. "I love you, Ma," he said out loud, prodded his horse, and rode off into the black of night.

CHAPTER ONE

SEPTEMBER 21, 1876

MENTRYVILLE, CALIFORNIA

Laughter burst out around the table.

James grabbed his glass and raised it. "To Alejandro Garcia, and to your family who came here many, many years ago. Thank you for your patience on this deal. I promise you we'll make your ancestors proud."

The other men assembled at the table besides Garcia were William Edington and Christopher Sheer, James' new partners in an oil company they had recently created. All raised their glasses. They clinked them together and cheered.

"Thank you, James, I agree, my grandfather would be proud. Now I just need to find a buyer for the other properties," Garcia lamented.

"Why not just hold onto them?" William said, placing his glass on the table and picking up his utensils.

A waiter had just dropped off steaks for each of them,

accompanied with roasted potatoes.

"William, my friend, I'm not getting any younger and I wish to move to Mexico City. With the proceeds of these sales, I'll have enough to buy a ranch and large house with many servants." Garcia laughed.

Taking a bottle of whiskey from the table, Christopher poured each man another drink then raised his glass. "Here's to having many servants!"

In unison the men cheered, "To many servants!"

They laughed and tossed the drinks back.

Garcia picked up a knife and fork and carved the thick meat on his plate. He stabbed the piece with his fork and put it into his mouth. As he chewed, he said, "James, tell me, what drives you?"

"What do you mean?" James asked, he too now cutting into his steak.

"Coming all this way from the middle of the country. Didn't you say you used to own a distillery?" Garcia asked, stuffing potato into his half-full mouth.

"Success," James answered. "I suppose I want to have more than my parents had."

"The elusive American dream, mentioned by many but found by few." Garcia laughed.

"Doesn't everyone want to get rich?" William asked. "I know James does, and I assume Christopher does too."

Christopher nodded in agreement.

"It's an American thing. In Mexico, we focus more on family, heritage, not wealth," Garcia explained.

"But, Alejandro, you're an American," James said.

"No, I was born when California was part of Mexico.

I didn't move, the border did," Garcia countered.

"But you're rich already. You never had nothing," William said.

Garcia shifted the food around on his plate as he thought about William's comment.

Around them the restaurant was filled with chatter and the sounds of people eating and drinking.

"I have been blessed, and I worked hard to expand what I was given, but now I'm tired. I'm an old man who now wishes to retire and move back to the nation of my birth. I'll leave the pursuit of wealth to you young Yanks," Garcia said.

"Don't call James here a Yank. His pa fought for the Confederacy," William said as he sliced off part of the fat from his meat.

"Is that so?" Garcia asked.

James gave William a hard stare, stirred in his chair and replied, "Yes, he fought and was killed. I can assure you I don't hold sympathies for the Confederacy or what they stood for. I'm a Union man."

Nodding, Garcia said, "Good to hear. We've had many of those rebels head into Mexico."

"I didn't know your pa was a rebel," Christopher said, his mouth open as he chewed.

Motioning that he should close his mouth, James said, "There's no need to talk about it since it wasn't me. That was my father's choice. I've decided to live a different life than him."

"That is true, we're not our fathers; we're independent men," Garcia said.

The waiter came to the table and asked, "How is the meal, Mr. Garcia?"

"It's good. Tell the cook he did a great job," Garcia said, rubbing his rotund belly.

"Shall I get another bottle of whiskey?" the waiter asked.

James hoped they wouldn't. He didn't want the night to turn into a party. He wished to get home to his wife, Emma, and his daughter, Scarlet.

"What do you gentlemen say?" Garcia asked.

"I could use more," William said.

"No more for me. Belinda will be expecting me within the next couple of hours, and I don't want—"

Patting him hard on the back, William blared, "He has a new bride at home whom he wishes to get back to and we all know why."

Red faced, Christopher lowered his head.

"Leave him alone, Will," James jabbed.

"What? It's true. He doesn't want to be too drunk," William howled.

Several heads turned to look.

Catching one person's gaze, William said, "Hello, sir, can I help you?"

The man quickly turned away.

Seeing that having another bottle would be nothing but trouble, James said, "Mr. Garcia, I think it's best we just finish what we have."

"I'll order another drink for myself and William here. You two can just drink water," Garcia said.

The waiter nodded and rushed off.

Leaving his elbows on the table, Garcia lowered his tone and said, "You'll bring the remainder of the money in two days; make it cash. Meet me at my office at eleven. My assistant, Maria, will be there and send you in to see me so we can finalize this deal."

Happy to hear the conversation had shifted back to work, James said, "We'll have the money and any documents you need to see."

"I don't need to see anything; just bring the money. We will all sign, and that will conclude our business unless you wish to buy some commercial buildings downtown, say the building you're currently leasing," Garcia said.

"Not at the moment, but could you give us a first right of refusal on the building we now lease from you?"

"James, this is your first right of refusal," Garcia shot back.

Wide-eyed, James said, "We're not in any position after acquiring this plot to buy the building," James said as he looked for affirmation from his partners.

"Very well. If you change your mind or if your circumstances change, let me know," Garcia said.

The men continued to talk casually, finished their meals, and got up from the table.

Christopher was the first to say his goodbyes, followed by William, who was headed to a gambling table.

Garcia and James talked as they walked out of the restaurant. Outside, both men paused before saying their goodbyes.

Breaking the silence, Garcia said, "You're confident about this land?"

"I am."

"When I asked you earlier what drove you, I think you gave me a half answer," Garcia said.

"A half answer?"

"Yes, you seem like a man out to prove something or that you're running away from something. I can't quite put my finger on it," Garcia said.

"Alejandro, I came from a poor family. My father was a farmer; he grew tobacco and didn't do that well at it. When he went off to fight the war, he left me and my mother with nothing. We tried to keep the farm going, but it was impossible, and his wages from the army, when they did come, were little. My poor mother was left to do work for several larger farm owners as a governess Then my father was killed. I vowed that I wouldn't be a father to my daughter that he was to me and that I wouldn't allow blind devotion to people or entities that in the end don't care for us. So maybe I'm both, I'm running away from that life as well as proving something."

Garcia stood, his hands in his pockets.

"Alejandro, thank you for the delicious dinner."

"You're welcome."

Putting out his hand, James said, "And thank you for the trust you have in us. We will take that land your family has had for generations and make it something that benefits the area and the people who live here."

Taking his hand, Garcia said, "Thank you. I'll see you and your partners in two days, then."

"In two days. Have a good night," James said.

Garcia turned and walked off into the darkness.

James stood on the walkway. He inhaled deeply then let it out. He couldn't believe he was on the cusp of acquiring over five hundred acres of land that he and his partners had confirmed had oil reservoirs below it. Soon they'd be drilling, and if all went as they hoped, they'd be one of the largest oil-producing companies in California.

Filled with hope and pride, he stepped off the walkway and headed for home.

PHOENIX, ARIZONA TERRITORY

Shooting up from a dead sleep, Rig scanned the darkened hotel room.

Laughter and sounds of revelry echoed through the wood floors from the bar and gambling hall below.

He wiped the sweat that glistened on his brow. He took a deep breath, then lowered himself back onto the thin mattress and laid his head on the pillow. Again he had been awakened from what he described as a dark dream.

These dark dreams weren't nightmares, they were more like visions. He pressed his eyes closed and focused on the faces he'd seen in the dark dream. He couldn't quite make them all out but two, both men. He could see them in his mind's eye committing horrible acts. These were not evil men; like most of his dark dreams, the people he saw were normal people acting in ways that made them bad, yet they could find redemption if they chose it.

A flash of a recent event including the men filled his mind, followed by a single name and a place.

Although he was tired, the urge to find and

confront these men pushed him to get out of bed. He got dressed, grabbed his gear, and exited the room, almost running into a woman who was clearly a prostitute.

"Hi, honey, can I…?" she asked flirtatiously until she saw the left side of his face. "Never mind," she said as she rushed off.

He shook his head and continued down the hall, passing rooms filled with hourly patrons. He slowly descended the stairs, passing more people who gave him the same horrified look once they saw the entire left side of his face was disfigured and scarred. In the lobby he went to the clerk, tossed him the key, and headed out into the cool night.

Like the bar and hotel, the street in front of him was filled with merrymaking individuals, all enjoying a night of libation and depravity.

He went to the livery and found the young boy who had helped him earlier in the day.

The boy got his horse and brought it to him. "He sure is a pretty color," the boy said, petting the uniquely colored red horse.

"His name is Fire," Rig said as he took a dollar gold coin from his vest pocket and gave it to the boy.

"What kind of horse is he? I've never seen one that looked quite like him," the boy said, rubbing his hand along the side of Fire.

"He's a rare beauty, a red roan," Rig said, taking the reins. He walked around the horse, adjusted the saddle, and stowed his gear in the saddlebags. "He looks happy. You took real good care of him, thank you."

"It was a pleasure, sir…say…"

Suspecting what he was about to ask, Rig said, "Go ahead. I get asked all the time."

"What happened to your face?" the boy asked.

"A fire ironically," Rig said, noting that his horse was called the very thing that had scarred him badly.

"A fire did that?" the boy asked, looking more closely.

Rig bent down and turned so that the light from a lantern close by could catch his face. "What does it look like?"

"Like the skin was melted," the boy said.

"That's exactly what happened," Rig said.

The boy found Rig's scars both revolting and interesting. He pulled back and asked, "Does it hurt?"

"No, in fact, I don't have any feeling in that side of my face," Rig said, poking it hard.

"What happened?"

"Long story, too long and grisly to tell you," Rig replied.

"Where are you heading?" the boy asked.

Rig thought for a second about his recent dark dream and answered, "Prescott, I'm off to Prescott."

"Why are you going there?" the boy asked.

"You certainly have many questions." Rig chuckled.

"I'm jealous is all. One day I want to see new places, get out of this town," the boy lamented.

Rig touched the top of the boy's head and closed his eyes.

The boy stood feeling a bit awkward, his eyes darting back and forth to see if anyone was watching.

Opening his eyes, Rig said, "You'll travel a lot when you're older, see many places, don't you worry."

"How do you know that?"

"Let's just say I have a way of knowing," Rig said with a crooked smile, the taut scarred skin pulling and distorting the left side of his face.

"I hope so," the boy said.

"Just keep being a good person, show kindness as often as you can, and help those in need; that'll be your ticket, trust me," Rig said.

"You coming back?"

Straddling Fire, Rig looked down and replied, "I don't know, but if I do, I'll see you then. Say, what's your name?"

"William Sebastian Gaudy, but everyone calls me Liam."

"Liam, my name is Rig and you already know Fire. You be well and do what I said."

"Yes, sir."

Rig tipped his hat and nudged Fire, who responded promptly.

The boy watched until they disappeared into the darkness.

CHAPTER TWO

SEPTEMBER 23, 1876

MENTRYVILLE, CALIFORNIA

When James entered the dining room, he expected to find Emma and Scarlet, but they weren't there, nor was breakfast sitting on the table like it normally was. Curious as to where they might be, he called out, "Emma." He could smell the distinct aroma of biscuits and bacon coming from the kitchen and now just assumed Emma was running late getting the food to the table. "Emma," he again called out.

Giggling came from the kitchen.

He walked to the door, pushed it open, and found Scarlet standing in the kitchen with an apron double wrapped around her waist so it would fit her small body. Standing next to her was Emma. "Sorry, we're almost ready."

"What's going on in here?" he asked with a big smile stretched across his face. It wasn't ordinary for Scarlet to be in the kitchen at this time.

Scooping a couple of eggs from a cast-iron skillet,

Emma replied, "Scarlet knew today was a big day for you, so she wanted to make breakfast herself. I'm just in here helping her finish it up."

Filled with joy at Scarlet's kind gift, he said, "You're very sweet, thank you, Scarlet."

"Go back and sit down, Papa. We'll have your favorite breakfast on the table in a jiffy," Scarlet said, her right cheek covered in flour.

"Okay, I'll do that," he said, going back to his spot at the dining table and taking a seat.

A minute later, the door swung open, and in came Scarlet holding a platter of fried eggs and bacon. She placed it in the center of the table and gave James a broad smile.

James took a deep breath and said, "Smells delicious."

"Just wait," she said and hurried off. She returned seconds later with a basket overflowing with steaming hot biscuits. She set them next to him and said, "And one more thing, actually two more things."

"Okay," he said happily.

Scarlet raced into the kitchen and came back just as fast with a plate of butter and a jar of strawberry jam. "You can't have biscuits without butter and jam."

"No, you can't," he said.

Emma appeared and said, "Scarlet, go wash up, hurry; then we'll all sit down."

Ever obedient, Scarlet ran back into the kitchen.

James reached out and took Emma's hand. "This is very nice, thank you."

"Don't thank me, thank your daughter. This was

her idea and she did most of the work," Emma replied.

"She'll make a good wife for someone," James said.

"Oh, let's not go talking about marrying her off so soon. She's only seven," Emma said. "Plus, maybe she'll want to follow in her father's footsteps and be in the oil business."

James chuckled. "Owning a single well isn't an oil business, but I do like the idea of her being an entrepreneur or taking over the family business."

"But you're opening a second well soon. What we have will grow," Emma reminded him.

Bouncing back in the room joyfully, Scarlet took her seat next to James and promptly took his hand. "Shall we say a prayer?" Scarlet was more religious than they were. They frequented church but more so because of societal norms and the fact that it looked well for James. However, when at home, they didn't discuss the Bible or pray much; this was what made Scarlet's affinity for it odd.

"Of course," James said.

Emma took her seat and the three joined hands. James led them in a quick prayer, then finished up as he said, "And Heavenly Father, thank you more importantly for my beautiful family. They bring me the greatest joy and happiness I could ever ask for." He cocked his head and gave Scarlet a quick wink.

She tried to return the wink but still hadn't mastered it; her face looked more like it was a spasm.

"This smells so good. Thank you, Scarlet, for this special meal," James said, taking the platter and scooping two eggs onto his plate.

"I thought you should start your day with some of your favorites," Scarlet replied.

"All of these are my favorites, especially the biscuits with butter and jam," he said.

"When do you meet with Mr. Garcia?" Emma asked.

"We have a meeting set for late this morning. There's nothing more to do but sign papers and pay him," James answered.

The meeting in question concerned the acquisition of a large parcel of land a few miles outside town. It was there James and his partners, William and Christopher, believed a large deposit of oil could be found.

Emma took James' hand and squeezed. "I'm proud of you."

"Thank you. I do this for us; I want us to be secure," he said.

"I know I wasn't quite sure about this move after all we did in Tucson, but now I see your vision," Emma said.

"Mama says you're a visionary, Papa. What does that mean?" Scarlet asked as she carefully applied butter on half of a biscuit.

"Well, a visionary is someone who can see where things might go in the future. They tend to know or can see what will be important or critical for mankind before others can. Now as far as me being one, that might be a stretch," he answered.

"Believe me, James Harris, you're a visionary. I still don't see how oil will be that important," Emma said.

"Emma my dear, we are on the cusp of many changes in industry, and I see oil playing a big role," James said.

"I can't argue. Our one well is doing great," Emma said, referring to the single well James had operating.

"So, tell me, what are you two doing today?" James asked.

"I'm going to school," Scarlet said.

"And how are you getting on with that boy Thomas since the altercation?" James asked.

"He's being nice to me now," Scarlet said.

"Good, remember, you can't strike out in anger. I know he was pinching you, but you must never turn to violence. There are better ways of dealing with our conflicts," James said.

"I know, Papa," she said.

"I don't want to keep beating a dead horse, but Scarlet was right to slap him. He was being cruel to her, and I believe her doing so is the reason he's now nice to her," Emma said.

"I know your viewpoint on this, Emma, but violence is never the way. Anyhow, let's talk about something else," James said, taking a biscuit from the basket.

"I'm meeting with Gwen, Priscilla and Emily; we're knitting socks for those less fortunate. Christmas will be upon us soon, and we thought it'd be nice if they have something during that special time of year," Emma said.

"Always thinking of others, that's why I love you," James said. He caught the time out of the corner of his eye and suddenly remembered he was to meet with his partners. "Oh my, look what time it is." He wiped his mouth and stood up from the table.

Shocked, Emma said, "But you don't go into the office until nine thirty."

"I forgot I was meeting with William and Christopher at nine. I apologize for the hasty departure; I'm sometimes shocked I don't forget to put my trousers on some days," James said.

Thinking quickly, Scarlet took the basket with the remaining biscuits and placed bacon, the plate of butter and the jar of jam inside. "This way you can finish and share with your friends."

He looked upon her with pride. "You're the sweetest and most thoughtful little girl in the world."

"They might be hungry too," Scarlet said.

With the basket in his hand, he rushed to the front door.

Emma followed right behind and stopped him just before exiting. She embraced him and said, "When you're finished, hurry home. I'm making a special dinner, and I'm baking a cake to celebrate."

"That's not necessary," he said.

"When good things happen for our family, we celebrate."

Kissing her, he asked, "How did I get you?"

"I don't know, but you're definitely lucky," she teased.

James gave Scarlet a quick kiss on the forehead and raced out the door.

PRESCOTT, ARIZONA TERRITORY

The doors of the saloon swung open and in stepped Rig. With each slow step he took, his spurs clanged. His eyes darted around the packed space, going from face to face. One thing he always made sure of when entering a new place was to ensure no one was about to draw on him.

All eyes were fixed on Rig and for good reason; besides his towering stature and wide build, many gawked at the left side of his face.

Rig reached the bar and paused. He looked left, then craned his head back and stared down the right side.

"What can I do for you?" the bartender asked, walking up to Rig.

Rig faced the bartender, took off his hat, and said, "Whiskey and information."

With Rig's hat now removed, the degree of disfigurement was even more noticeable. His short-cropped hair was patchy on the top of his head due to the thick scars that crisscrossed it.

The bartender cringed at the sight. "Whiskey it is," he said, turning away to grab a bottle. He spun back, set it in front of Rig, pulled the cork and poured. Just as he was about to cork it and take it back, Rig said, "Just leave the bottle."

"Yes, sir," the bartender said. "That'll be three dollars."

Rig reached into his vest pocket and removed three gold dollar coins and tossed them on the bar, followed by a ten-dollar piece. "I need information too."

The bartender took the coins, including the eagle, and asked, "What sort of information do you need?"

"If you're looking for where they sell bags to cover that ugly mug, go to Sherry's General Store!" A drunkard at the far end of the bar howled in laughter.

No one in the bar laughed at the joke; instead they grew more tense, as they now sensed a fight was about to occur.

Rig leered in the direction of the drunkard. While he was used to this sort of treatment, he didn't like it.

"Damn, you're an ugly son of a bitch," the drunkard howled. "Look at him, y'all, he looks as if he fell out of the ugly tree and hit every branch on the way down!"

"Clem, just keep your piehole shut! I don't need you hurling insults at my customers," the bartender barked.

Ignoring Clem, Rig turned to the bartender and asked, "Your customers? Is this establishment yours?" In his dream he'd seen this bar and saw that the man he needed to talk to owned it.

"Yes, sir, it is," the bartender said.

"Then you're the man I'm here to see," Rig said. His right hand shifted towards his holstered Colt Buntline.

The bartender's eyes widened as he took a cautious few steps away from Rig. "Me?"

"Are you Philip Nance?" Rig asked.

The drunkard stumbled over and shouted, "Is this ugly son of a bitch causing you trouble?"

With his left hand, Rig pulled an eight-inch-long knife from a sheath on his belt and held it straight out, the tip just a hair from the drunkard's throat. Without looking at him, he said, "I suggest you stop right there."

The drunkard froze, knowing his life was on the line. "Don't stab me."

"Answer the question. Are you Philip Nance?" Rig asked the bartender.

The bartender raised his hands as if surrendering and replied, "No, I'm not him. I bought this place from him just a couple of days ago."

"Are you lying to me?" Rig asked. His dreams, while mostly accurate, were hard to decipher sometimes. This appeared to be one of those times.

"No, mister, I'm not," the bartender said, gulping loudly.

"He's not Phil; that mean old codger sold him this place. He's Conrad," the drunkard said, his tone now noticeably more congenial.

Rig looked deeply into Conrad's eyes and said, "Where can I find Philip Nance?"

"I'll tell you, but can you first lower your knife from Clem's throat?" Conrad asked. "And take your hand off the back strap of your pistol?"

Rig craned his head in Clem's direction and replied, "Only if he agrees to walk away and not say another mean word again."

"I will, I promise," Clem whined.

Rig lowered the knife slowly and slid it back in its sheath. "Now, where can I find Philip Nance?"

Conrad told the man everything he knew.

Satisfied with the information he'd received, Rig took a few quick shots of his whiskey, nodded, then put his hat back on. "Good day to you all." He spun around and walked towards the door.

"Say, mister, what's your name?" Conrad asked.

Rig reached the door, glanced over his shoulder, and replied, "I've gone by many names, but to Philip Nance, I'm justice."

MENTRYVILLE, CALIFORNIA

James examined the plot map carefully one more time. Once the deal was finalized, he and his partners could potentially have the largest oil-producing patch in the state to date. For James the allure of oil was new. Upon hearing oil had been discovered in the Santa Susana Mountains, north of Los Angeles, he saw the future. Not hesitating one second, he'd packed the family's bags and departed Arizona territory for Mentryville, California.

His journey to California had taken him eleven years and many miles. Since leaving Missouri in 1865, he'd bounced around doing odd jobs, mostly labor at first, until he met a man by the name of Colin Herring in Colorado Territory. He had been working for one of Colin's businesses and caught his eye. The two slowly became friends. Over the next couple of years, Colin taught him the most valuable thing he'd ever learned about becoming rich, and that was a man could never grow wealthy selling the hours of his day. He taught him that if he ever sought riches, he'd need people working for him and to have a product that was in demand twenty-four hours per day. James heeded that advice and, upon leaving his job, went to Tucson, Arizona Territory, and opened up a distillery. His reason: of all the cities he had done research on, Tucson imported all of its spirits, leaving an industry that was wide open to exploit. It was here that he met Emma, and within a year they were married.

The distillery took a while to get off the ground, but through hard work and determination, it grew. The income he generated from it wasn't great, but James could say he was better off than most. However, for James that wasn't enough; he wanted more. After celebrating Scarlet's sixth birthday, he met a man in passing at a saloon he sold his whiskey to. As the two chatted, James came to discover the man was passing through. When he asked where the man was headed, the man replied, "California to find black gold." Needless to say the comment got James' attention. After several hours of questions directed at the man, James could see the potential. Up until then, the main oil being produced in California was to the north, with only small sites in the south, but none of what was coming out of the ground in California was enough to quench the thirst for the growing demand. This fit the formula for James.

He went directly home that night and told Emma he was selling the distillery and moving the family to Southern California. Within a week he'd sold his distillery to a local saloon owner, packed the family into several covered wagons, and moved west. In the span of a year, he had one operating well that was producing two barrels of oil per day; he was officially an oilman. Now he was close to expanding his share of the market by going into business with William and Christopher, who were both like him, operators of their own single wells nearby.

"The surveyors told me they've seen oil percolating on the top of the ground. Can you believe it? It's so damn plentiful that it's seeping out of the ground," William said happily.

James stoically replied, "It's not our land until we sign the deal. Now, where is Christopher?"

"He's at the bank, ensuring the money is ready to transfer," William said.

"He's late. I pray all is well," James said, pulling out his pocket watch to see if the time corresponded to the clock on the wall.

"He's fine. Maybe he stopped by to see his new bride." William laughed as he gave James a wink.

"There's no time for that," James said, his tone indicating his serious demeanor.

"Live a little, James. Everything doesn't have to be so critical," William jabbed.

Giving him a stern look, James said, "I'm usually the one who doesn't find stress in most things, but this moment is critical. We're on the cusp of finalizing a deal that could give us a significant hold on oil production in California. So right now is not a time for jokes or for Christopher stopping off to see Belinda."

"I was saying that in jest. I can't imagine he's paying her a visit," William said, his smile turning to a frown.

Pivoting back to business, James asked, "You have all the documents, including our incorporation paperwork?"

Patting a satchel, William answered, "All right here."

"Good."

"Can you believe it? Soon Pacific Star Oil Works will officially be the owner of that parcel and hopefully within a year be producing upwards of fifty barrels per day," William said joyfully.

"I can see it, for sure, but like I said, let's not get ahead of ourselves," James said as he rolled up the map. He cinched it tight with a piece of twine and set it on his desk. He arranged other documents and placed them in a leather case. Removing his watch once more, he checked the time. "Where on earth is he?"

"We've got time," William said. "And don't be so negative. Old man Garcia likes us; we had dinner with him the other night. The deal is all but sealed."

"We need to meet Mr. Garcia in fifteen minutes—" James said, his teeth clenched from the anticipation of what was close to happening.

"And it takes five minutes to get to his office. We'll be fine," William said, interrupting James.

James paced back and forth.

"Now you're making me nervous," William said, his feet kicked up on a desk as he fiddled with a deck of playing cards.

Just as James was about to counter William, he spotted Christopher racing towards the office. "Something's wrong."

"Stop saying that, we—"

"No, there's something wrong. Christopher is sprinting this way, and the look on his face says it all," James snapped. He ran to the front door and threw it open.

William hopped to his feet, spotted Christopher too

and, like James, could see the concern written all over his partner's face.

"It's gone, it's gone," Christopher said, entering the office, his face red with beads of sweat on his brow.

"What do you mean?" James asked, slamming the door shut.

"He sold it," Christopher exclaimed.

"What do you mean he sold it?" James asked.

Taking a deep breath, Christopher slowed his breathing and said, "I was leaving the bank; I saw Mr. Garcia talking to two other men; then he waved for me to come over. I thought he merely wanted to say good morning, but that wasn't it. He proceeded to tell me that he'd sold the land to someone else."

"Did you ask why?" James asked.

"Even though I was overcome with shock, I did ask him why," Christopher explained.

"He can't do that," William barked in anger, pounding his fist onto the desk.

"Let Christopher speak. Now please continue," James said, admonishing William.

"He said another offer, a time-sensitive one, came in not an hour ago. I asked why he didn't give us the chance to counter, and he said that the other offer was so good that there was no need to even discuss it with us," Christopher explained.

James walked to the front door, snatched his hat from a peg near the door, and threw the door open.

"Where are you going?" William cried out.

James donned his hat, turned and replied, "I'm going

to talk to Mr. Garcia."

William leapt to his feet and raced towards the door. "I'm coming with you."

"Stay here. I'll be back soon," James said.

"I'm an equal partner and demand a seat at the table. Plus I intend on giving him a piece of my mind if he doesn't allow us to buy the parcel," William barked.

"You're going nowhere, and you won't be giving anyone a piece of your mind. Mr. Garcia has made an error, but he's also a highly respected figure in the area; it's best we stay on his good side," James said.

"Why are you not willing to fight for this?" William crowed.

"I'm going to see him to make our case, but if he's made up his mind, then that's it, we regroup and try something else," James explained. "And don't preach to me about fighting for this. I put this deal together; I brought you two in. I want this more than you can know. I'm willing to do what I can, but acting emotional won't change it. Alejandro is a reasonable man and doesn't respond to outbursts of rage."

Turning to Christopher, William asked, "What do you think? We should go with him."

"Will, James put this together from the start. Let him go. If anyone here can turn this around, it's him," Christopher answered in his usual soft-spoken tone.

Frustrated, William tossed his hat on the desk and frowned. "Fine, but you hurry directly back as soon as you have any news."

"Of course, where else would I go?" James asked.

"And if he doesn't budge, I want our deposit back immediately," William snapped. He walked back to his chair and sat down. "And I mean immediately!"

"Just have faith," James said then hurried off.

PRESCOTT, ARIZONA TERRITORY

Rig rode to the exact location where Conrad told him Philip would be and dismounted. He looked at the small cabin tucked into the side of the rocky hill and knew that someone was there due to the horse hitched out front and the plume of smoke that rose from the chimney. He walked up to the door and knocked.

"Who's there?" a craggy voice called out. It was Philip Nance and he didn't want to see anyone, especially someone he didn't know.

"I'm here to see Philip Nance," Rig replied calmly.

"There's no one here by that name," Nance shouted.

Rig pressed his eyes closed for a brief second, mumbled something unintelligible, then opened them wide. Not hesitating another second, he kicked in the door and entered the small one-room cabin.

"Who the hell do you think you are?" Nance asked, jumping up from the small table in the center of the space.

Rig drew his Colt, cocked it and said, "You're Philip Nance and we need to talk."

Looking down the barrel of the pistol, Nance threw up his arms and yelled, "Don't shoot."

"Step away from the table. Keep your hands above your head," Rig said.

Nance did as he said.

"Take a seat in that chair," Rig said, motioning towards a small armless chair next to the fireplace.

It was apparent Nance wasn't prepared to encounter anyone, as he was wearing long underwear, which were filthy and soiled. He sat in the chair and asked, "Who are you?"

"That doesn't matter. I'm here to ask you a few questions and to help you," Rig said.

"Help me? You call kicking in my door helping? So what is it, what do you want?" Nance asked.

"Weeks ago you orchestrated a scheme that left several families without their life savings. Do you confess to that?" Rig asked.

Nance's eyes widened when hit with the question. He couldn't keep from staring at Rig's heavily scarred face. "Who are you?"

"Do you confess to doing that?" Rig asked, the pistol leveled at Nance's grimy and stubbled face.

"Who sent you? Huh? Was it Crawford?"

"Is that a confession?" Rig asked.

"Who are you?"

"You're leaving me with few options here. Now confess, and after that we can figure out a way for you to repent for your sins," Rig said.

"Are you talking about those damn Irish who thought they could come into town and take over?"

"Do you or do you not confess to stealing their money?" Rig asked.

"You can't call taking money from rich people

stealing. Those Micks strolled into my saloon and acted like they owned the place. I merely concocted a way to have them part with a small amount," Nance spat.

"You took their life savings. You stole, and now they're left homeless," Rig said, recalling his dream.

"That's a lie," Nance hollered.

"It's true, I saw it," Rig said confidently.

"You're a damn liar!" Nance barked.

"Mr. Nance, do you confess to your sins?" Rig asked.

"Yes, I took those people's money."

"Good, you've confessed. Now are you willing to repent?" Rig asked.

"Who sent you?" Nance asked. "Was it one of those families?"

"No, it was someone greater than them. Again, are you willing to repent?" Rig asked.

Nance nodded and said, "Yes."

"Good," Rig said. He uncocked his pistol and holstered it. "I need you to give me all the money back."

"What?"

"Part of your repentance is to give me the money back. I'll make sure it gets back to the rightful owners," Rig said.

"Oh, I see, you're here to steal it from me," Nance yelped.

"I can assure you I'm not here to steal it. If I were, I wouldn't have been talking to you, I would've gunned you down," Rig said.

"Well, I don't have it."

"Give me what you have, and we'll work out a

contract for you to pay back the rest," Rig said.

"Who the hell do you think you are?" Nance barked. "Huh, are you the law?"

"It doesn't matter who I am or who sent me. Now, are you willing to repay what you stole?"

Nance remained silent as he pondered attacking Rig. He glanced to the table and saw a fork sitting on the table.

Rig cocked his head and said, "I know what you're thinking, and it won't work out well for you."

"And what am I thinking?" Nance asked.

"You're thinking you can grab that fork and stab me before I can draw on you. I'm here to tell you that won't work out well for you," Rig said calmly.

"Is that so," Nance said arrogantly.

"I'm not here to kill you, but if I have to, I will, and then you'll be sent on your way to hell," Rig said. "And I'm trying to prevent that."

"Hell?" Nance laughed. "Listen, I was already slated to go to hell, so your threats of the afterlife don't disturb me."

"Don't do it," Rig said, sensing that Nance was about to go for the fork.

"You won't get my money," Nance said just before leaping towards the table. He snatched the fork and lunged towards Rig.

Just as Rig had warned, he stepped back, drew, cocked the pistol, and fired a single shot, which struck Nance in the face, just below his left eye.

Nance dropped to the floor dead.

Rig sighed, uncocked the pistol, holstered it, and

knelt down next to Nance's body. He rolled him onto his back and sighed. "I warned you."

Nance's eyes were open in a deathly stare towards the ceiling.

Rig closed Nance's eyes then dipped his thumb into some blood and marked Nance's forehead with a cross. "You were wrong, you weren't destined for Hell, but now you've lost that opportunity." He stood up and searched the cabin for the money. He found a lockbox with an amount that equaled half of what Nance had stolen and took it. He strapped the box to his saddlebags and mounted his horse. He looked up towards the sky and said, "I tried. Some people just never learn."

MENTRYVILLE, CALIFORNIA

James wasn't nervous about the conversation he was about to have with Mr. Garcia. On the contrary, he had a sense of confidence that the outcome was going to go his way, like it often did.

A young Mexican woman opened the office door and said, "Ah, Mr. Harris, good day; Mr. Garcia is expecting you."

James smiled and said, "Is he?"

The young woman, her black silky hair pulled back tight in a bun, returned his smile and said, "Yes, he is."

James stepped past her and into the darkened office space. He was familiar with the office after having spent many hours negotiating the deal. Seeing Mr. Garcia in his usual chair, James called out, "Alejandro, you knew I was coming, so let's get down to brass tacks. You know why I'm here."

Garcia's attention was focused out a large window that overlooked the main street and the mountains beyond. Without turning to face James, he said, "My grandparents came to California long before you Americans took it."

Not sure how to respond, James sat down in a small chair in front of the desk and remained quiet.

"Today I was provided an offer that I told your partner I couldn't pass up. I normally don't conduct myself the way I did today. You see, never in my life have I shook hands with a man and then gone back on that handshake…until this morning," Garcia said, his gaze still looking out towards the mountains to the east.

"Alejandro, that is what I'd like to discuss with you. I'm hoping my partners and I still have an opportunity to acquire the land," James said.

Garcia replied, "I pride myself on being fair, honest and having integrity; my grandfather told me long ago when I was a boy that a man's reputation is his greatest asset. You can spend a life doing great things and building up your reputation, but if you make one bad decision, run afoul morally, all those years of effort are destroyed. Some say that's not just, that all men should be given a second chance, and I agree with that to a certain degree. All men should have second chances, but their sins should be known so that other men know whom they're doing business with."

"What is the problem? I fear you're alluding to something. I'd prefer you just come out and tell me why you didn't sell us the parcel as we all agreed upon," James said, finally growing impatient with the cryptic talk and sensing that for the first time in a long time he wasn't going to win out.

Garcia spun around and replied, "It came to my attention this morning that I was selling that parcel of land to a murderer."

James recoiled from the accusation. "Murderer? I don't understand what you're claiming."

Placing his elbows firmly on his desk and leaning in, Garcia said, "You, Mr. Harris, murdered women and children."

Understanding what now was happening, James asked, "Who told you this?"

"Three weeks ago two men made my acquaintance. They expressed interest in the same parcel. When I told them we had a deal and that I had even taken a deposit on it, they went away. They came back yesterday to give me the news about your past crimes. At first I didn't believe it, so I telegrammed the sheriff in the county where you used to reside, and inquired. I received his reply this morning. It appears you were never officially charged with murder, but many feel you're partly to blame for the deaths of two women and three children. The two gentlemen clarified what happened to me this morning after I summoned them. They detailed to me that you took it upon yourself to burn the domicile. Is that true?"

"Who told you these lies?" James said. He could feel the anger he often kept tamped down rising.

"So you're denying it?" Garcia asked.

49

"Who?" James again asked.

"Tell me, Mr. Harris, did you or did you not kill women and children after the war?" Garcia asked.

Not wanting to explode with the same anger that had caused him so much angst years ago, James promptly stood up and said, "I fear you believe these men over me, and I don't know what else to say to you except that I am not guilty of murder."

"Did you kill those people?" Garcia pressed.

"Mr. Garcia, I am deeply upset that we cannot complete the transaction that we all agreed upon. I expect you'll return the deposit right away," James said, as he felt his temper rising..

"I think you should know that I cannot in good conscience do business with a man like you," Garcia said.

"I'm not the man you describe," James countered.

"You may not be now, but the question is, were you?" Garcia said.

"We have all done things that we regret, but I'm not a murderer, that I can assure you," James said.

"That's not what these men told me. They said you specifically described murdering those innocent people, women and little children."

"I pray you'll reconsider because the story that I murdered people is false," James insisted.

"Then you say you weren't responsible for anyone's death?" Garcia again asked.

Clenching his hat tightly, James replied, "Alejandro, things happened years ago that were regretful. It can be only be defined as a fog of war, but I never murdered anyone," James said, finally alluding to the killings.

"Then you did kill innocents, hmm," Garcia said, his head bobbing up and down as he pondered. "Mr. Harris, the parcel is now gone; there's no getting it back. I liked you, I really did. I was hoping we could do other business, but I cannot now."

"Please make sure the deposit is returned promptly, and thank you for your time," James said and hastily spun around.

"One more thing, I do not plan on telling anyone about this or what you've done. It is not my place but yours to be honest with whomever you conduct business with," Garcia said.

Unable to reply, James said, "Good day." He threw open the door and hurried through the lobby until he reached the front door. When he reached for it, he paused as he caught sight of his trembling hand. Who was Mr. Garcia referring to? Who had shown up from his past all the way in California? He needed to know and planned on finding out who had just orchestrated an assassination on his reputation. He steadied his hand, grabbed the knob, turned it and opened the door. The cool air hit his face. Putting on his hat, he exited the office and went out onto the walkway. He contemplated telling his partners the truth but wasn't sure if that was what he should do. He feared if he told them why Mr. Garcia had reneged on the deal, that would only unravel his life even further. He knew William would overreact, and by the end of the day the entire town would know. If Mr. Garcia meant what he'd said about not telling anyone, then he could lie to his partners and try to recover from this. But the one thing that hung over his head was who had told Garcia, and were they planning to tell others?

Determined to repair the damage, he headed back to his office to tell his partners that the land was gone, but would not tell them why.

***

After breaking the news to his partners, James left the office and went directly home. He walked up to the front door but hesitated before going inside. How was he going to explain this to his wife, Emma? He knew she was planning on baking a cake for the special occasion to celebrate the acquisition of the land, but now he'd have to tell her it wasn't going to happen. Was he going to lie to her too? he asked himself. Of course, he'd have to on account that he never told her about the incident in Missouri. Telling her now would no doubt leave her questioning what else he might be hiding. Upon leaving the house earlier that day, he never would have guessed that this would be where he was. Never did he imagine his past would come back to haunt him so.

The door flew open, and there standing before him was Emma, an apron wrapped around her waist. "James, what are you doing standing here?"

Sheepishly he replied, "I was thinking, nothing more." He stepped inside and put his briefcase on a chair in the foyer.

She closed the door and walked up to him. "You head upstairs, get freshened up, and come down to the parlor. I've opened a bottle of brandy. I thought we could both—"

He took her by the hands but couldn't look her in the eyes.

Not only sensing something was wrong, she could see he was visibly disturbed. "James, what's happened?"

"We lost the land," he blurted out.

"How? What changed?" she asked, shocked by the news.

"It's a long story, but Mr. Garcia sold the parcel to someone else," James said without telling the total truth.

"Oh no, why would he do that?"

"It's just business."

"That's not business, that's underhanded. He's a scoundrel," she seethed.

"No, he's not, he's just a businessman who had a better deal cross his desk at the last minute. Now, sweetheart, I don't need you to be worried about this. We'll be fine. We'll find another parcel so we can expand, but until then we'll keep our enterprise humming along. We've been blessed with what we have, and we should just thank God that we have what we have at the moment," he said.

She lowered her head, stepped closer, and wrapped her arms around him. With her head buried in his chest, she could hear his heartbeat. "You're so right. We are blessed and I need to trust that you'll take care of us, as you always have. I just had high hopes for what that land could do for us."

James caressed her. He was grateful for her and didn't know what he'd do if he lost her.

Scarlet stuck her head in the room and cried out, "Papa, you're home." She raced towards them with her arms open wide.

Seeing her brought a smile to James' face. "How's my sweetheart?"

Scarlet wrapped her arms around them both and said, "Family hug."

The three held each other like they often did.

James' thoughts quickly went back to the events of the day and his secret being exposed. What would happen if Emma found out? He then went through the scenario of him confessing the horrible event. When he did, it didn't sound so bad. He had only been sixteen at the time and he had been lied to, but she would no doubt question why he'd kept such a thing hidden for so long. He was more than embarrassed by what had happened. The reason he kept it a secret was due to the fact that he actually believed he was guilty. Of course, he didn't feel he was the sole party in what had happened, but he definitely held himself partly responsible. Many times he'd run that night over and over in his head. When he'd seen the children, he should have just dropped the torches, turned and ran home. Why hadn't he? None of this would be haunting him now if he had just done that.

"Come, let's go sit and enjoy a glass of brandy," Emma said, taking James by the hand.

"But you opened it to celebrate," he said.

"We have so much to celebrate, dear. We love each

other, we have beautiful Scarlet, and we have a wonderful home."

Her thoughtful and sweet words almost brought him to tears.

Seeing his emotional state, she again embraced him. "James, this is just an obstacle on our journey. There's not a thing that can stop us."

"Papa, you look sad," Scarlet said, hugging him, her small arms wrapped around his waist.

"I'm disappointed is all. I had high hopes for what was going to happen with that land," he said.

"Like you said, there will be another piece of land. We'll be fine," Emma said.

"Emma, do you love me unconditionally?" he asked suddenly.

Hearing the surprising question, she paused.

"I mean…will you always love me no matter what?" he asked.

"This entire business has you thinking all sorts of odd. Of course I'll always love you. You're the nicest, gentlest and kindest man I've ever met. What you've done in business only adds to us, but that could be taken away tomorrow and I'd be just fine. I'd give this house away and move into a shack as long as you were there to share it with me," she answered.

A tear came to his eye; he quickly wiped it away.

"You are very upset. I've never seen you like this. Husband, come and sit down, relax. . I almost have a mind to go down to see Mr. Garcia and give him a piece of my mind," Emma said, escorting James to one of two wingback chairs that sat in front of the fireplace.

"Don't do that," he snapped.

Shocked by his curt response, she said, "I would never interject myself into your business. I'm merely explaining that I feel strongly about it."

"He and I could still do business down the road," James lied, nestling into the chair.

"You'd do business with a man like that?" Emma asked.

Scarlet brought over the silver tray that held the decanter of brandy and two glasses. "Here, Papa."

"Thank you, sweetheart," James said. He turned to Emma and continued, "One must never burn bridges in business."

"Seems like he burned the bridge not you," Emma said.

"Sweet wife, can we now stop talking about it?"

"Yes, of course," she said.

"And can you please take a seat next to me? Oh, Scarlet, since we're celebrating, why don't you go fetch a bottle of root beer or sarsaparilla," James said.

"Before dinner?" Emma asked.

"We're celebrating as a family, aren't we? Scarlet should enjoy something too," James said.

Emma nodded.

"Oh, thank you, Papa." Scarlet squealed as she raced out of the room.

"You spoil her," Emma said.

"No, I just love on her, like I do you," James said.

Scarlet returned with a small glass of root beer. She sat

in a small curved love seat opposite them, a large smile stretched across her tiny face.

James and Emma had poured their brandies and each had a glass in their hands.

Holding his up high, James said, "A toast to the Harris family, may God continue to bless us with love, health and good fortune."

"Cheers," Emma and Scarlet said in unison.

The three touched glasses then drank.

As the sweet liquor touched James' lips, he said a prayer to himself that his secret would stay just that...a secret.

CHAPTER THREE

SEPTEMBER 24, 1876

MENTRYVILLE, CALIFORNIA

James, Emma and Scarlet enjoyed a nice breakfast. Upon finishing, Emma excused herself and promptly left the house to go to a sewing group she'd been meeting weekly. This left James and Scarlet at home by themselves.

Wanting to get back to work, James went to his office and began to go over maps of the surrounding area with hopes of spotting another parcel that could serve him and his partners. He was determined after a good night's rest to get back to securing his vision for the new oil company.

As his eyes scanned a map of the San Fernando Valley, a knock was heard at the front door. He lifted his head and wondered who might be there, as they weren't expecting any company. "Scarlet, I'll get it," he cried out.

Scarlet was in her bedroom upstairs reading. "Okay, Papa."

James went to the door, opened it and, upon seeing who it was, almost fainted.

"Well, if it isn't James Harris, the coward of Missouri," Cecil said just before spitting tobacco juice on the front porch.

Next to him was John Kemp. John tipped his hat and said, "Mr. Harris, a pleasure to see you again."

"It was you," James howled.

"Are you referring to your failed acquisition with Mr. Garcia?" John asked rhetorically.

"You lied to him; you said I murdered those people. You know I didn't do that," James barked.

Scarlet overheard the loud voices and came to the top of the stairs and listened.

Angry, James barked, "You lied and destroyed that deal."

"On the contrary, we told him the truth as you told it then. You stood before me and Cecil and declared that you had, and these are your words, 'murdered those people.'"

Recalling that he had said those very words, James backtracked, "I was angry; I misspoke. Was I there? Yes. Did I murder those people? No. I—"

Interrupting James, John said, "You only killed them? If that makes you feel better, then so be it, but many people would see it differently."

"You made me," James snapped.

Cecil spit again and asked, "Aren't you going to invite us in?"

Noticing that their conversation could be in earshot of Scarlet, James motioned for them to move, then stepped out on the front porch, closing the door behind him with a thud. "What are you doing at my house?"

"We're here to make you a deal," John said.

"What more can you want from me? You took that parcel," James said.

"You see, James, do you mind if I call you by your first name?" John asked, feigning courtesy.

"What do you want? Is it money? Fine, I'll give you money, but then you need to move on, leave me and my family in peace," James said.

"We want a lot from you. We really want the years we lost in a Missouri prison back," John said.

"You were imprisoned? Well, it seems you might have deserved that," James growled.

John cleared his throat and looked away.

"Let me kill him, please, John," Cecil said, pulling his jacket back to reveal his holstered Colt Single Action Army.

John waved at Cecil to stop. Looking up at James, he continued, "We were arrested for the crime you committed, James. No doubt we tried to explain that we hadn't done it, but it didn't matter. The Yankee authorities, along with their quivering sympathizers we used to call fellow Missourians, had us jailed. We came close to being hanged, but they felt killing us would only embolden the resistance, so we served nine years in a filthy jail cell," John said.

"What do you want?" James again asked.

"We want payback. You owe us," John said.

"You want money? Tell me how much," James asked. He was willing to give them whatever they wanted so he could be rid of them.

"We want to take your life away from you," John

clarified.

Raising his arms, James shouted, "Then shoot me; go ahead, kill me. Go ahead, Cecil, pull that pistol and gun me down."

"We're not here to kill you; we're here to take everything you've created away from you, one piece at a time. The first was that land; the next, well, we'll see what that is. We mainly came here to say hello and to let you know we're now in the oil business and that we're not going anywhere. We're here to stay, and soon enough we just might own this town, but of course, that all depends on if we can make some deals," John said.

"You'll get nothing from me. Do you hear me? Nothing," James shouted.

"You don't have leverage, James, so stop acting like you do," John said.

"You'll get nothing from me. Now get off my porch!" James shouted. He rarely showed anger or emotion, but here it was on full display.

"Why won't you let me kill him? I'd enjoy that more. I've been counting the days until I saw this coward," Cecil seethed.

Turning to Cecil, John said, "We're killing him, just slower." Facing James again, he continued, "Maybe the wife will be here next time we come and pay a visit. I'd love to meet her."

Cecil chuckled.

James clenched his fists and shouted, "Off my porch."

"What will you do? Contact the sheriff? Please do. Tell him who we are and why we're here," John said.

"I'm surprised he's not pissing himself; you, boy, have grown a pair to talk to John Kemp the way you are," Cecil said. "Please, John, let's just take him around back and hang him…slowly."

Putting a gentle hand on Cecil's shoulder, John said, "I told you a long time ago, we'll get our due, but I want it to be so painful—not physical pain, but emotional. I want James here to suffer." Facing James again, he continued, "And if you think about leaving, we'll find you. We won't let up."

"Mr. Garcia contacted the sheriff in Platte County. There is no warrant for my arrest, so your threat is meaningless. I could contact the local sheriff, and he'll—" James declared before being interrupted.

"And you'll tell him what? That we out-negotiated you?" John asked.

"Leave!" James shouted.

The door behind James opened, and there stood Scarlet. "Papa, why are you yelling?"

Seeing the girl, John knelt down and asked, "What's your name, precious?"

"My name is Scarlet. Are you friends with my papa?"

"I wouldn't say friends, but we've known each other a long time," John said with a devilish smile.

Lowering his voice, James said calmly, "You two need to go, now."

Ignoring James, John continued, "Do you love your papa?"

Scarlet nodded.

"Then tell him he has to do whatever we tell him going

forward," John said.

Scarlet tugged at James' pant leg and asked, "Papa, what does he mean?"

"Leave," James said.

John stood upright, gave James a smile, and said, "We'll be seeing you soon, I'm sure of it."

James seethed.

Cecil and John exited the porch, got on their horses, and rode away.

James turned, quickly picked up Scarlet, and went inside, locking the door behind him.

"Papa, who were those men?" Scarlet asked.

"I want you to promise me something, can you do that? Can you make a promise to Papa?"

Scarlet nodded.

"This is our secret; you must not tell Mama about these men. Do you understand?"

She nodded again.

"Do you promise?"

"Are those men bad?"

"They're not nice, know that, but Mama must not know they were here or anything they said," James said.

"Are you going to give them something?" she asked.

"No, I'm not giving them anything. Remember what happened to you at school with Thomas?"

Scarlet nodded.

"This is similar…"

"Did they pinch you?" Scarlet asked innocently.

"No, but they're bullying me and I won't stand for it," James said.

"Are you going to tell a teacher or someone like that?"

"No, but I will stand up for myself."

"Are you going to sock him?" Scarlet asked, raising her clenched fists.

"Not like that…anyway, can you promise me you won't say a word?"

"I won't tell Mama. It's our secret," she said. "But can you tell me if—"

"Enough questions, just know that you can't say a thing to your mother," James again pressed.

"Okay," Scarlet replied, nodding her head sweetly. As she thought about what she'd seen and more importantly heard, her face scrunched. "I'm worried about you, Papa. You don't look happy."

"I'm fine," he replied.

"I'm worried about you, I'm scared that you're upset, and I don't know what to do," Scarlet confessed.

"Know how you can help? Don't say a word and—"

"Pray, I'll go pray for you. I'll pray that those bad men go away, that they don't hurt you or Mama," she said.

"Thank you, Scarlet, that's sweet. Now run upstairs and go back to reading," James said.

Scarlet jogged off, stopped at the base of the stairs, and turned. "Papa, I'm going to go up and pray for you to be happy and for those bad men to leave you alone."

Her words brought tears to his eyes. "You do that, sweetheart, thank you."

Scarlet raced back upstairs, knelt beside her bed, and began to pray.

PRESCOTT, ARIZONA TERRITORY

Rig woke suddenly; his eyes stared at the textured ceiling above him. Sweat glistened on his skin, with several beads running down from his brow. He sat up and looked around the small hotel room.

The sun's early light peeked through the sides and bottom of the drawn blind, illuminating just enough for him to see.

He pivoted his legs out from underneath the sheet and placed them on the cool wood floor. He'd had another dream; in this one he saw several men and a young girl. The girl was pleading, begging for someone to come save her and her family.

He got to his feet, stretched, and walked to the dresser. He dipped his hands into a bowl of cool water and splashed his face. Putting his weight against it, he leaned in and stared at his reflection in the mirror. Like he often did, he cocked his head so he only saw the side of his face that wasn't scarred. He wondered what he'd look like if he'd never been injured those many years ago. Would he be married? Have children? He'd ponder these questions then quickly push them from his thoughts, as it didn't matter. He was destined to live the life he was leading.

The image of a little girl popped in his mind again. She was in need and scared.

He got dressed, grabbed his gear, and headed down to the hotel lobby.

Upon seeing him, the clerk, a young man named Kyle, said, "Good morning, sir."

Rig turned so he fully faced Kyle and said, "Mornin'."

Kyle recoiled upon seeing Rig's face completely, putting his gaze back on the ledger before him.

Rig shook his head and smiled. He'd grown accustomed to this type of response. Needing some information, he headed towards the clerk but was stopped when a small boy approached him. After hundreds of encounters, he knew what was about to occur.

"What happened to your face?" the boy asked.

Rig looked down and said, "I was burned."

"Did it hurt?"

"I don't remember."

"It looks like that side of your face was melted," the boy said.

"Because it was."

"Can I touch it?" the boy asked, genuinely curious.

Rig looked around but saw no one around who resembled the boy's parents. He bent down and said, "Sure."

The boy touched it and said, "It's smooth. I thought it would feel rough."

"You would think that, right?" Rig said.

"Joshua Paul Givens, what are you doing?" a woman howled from the adjacent dining hall located in a wing of the lobby.

The boy pulled his hand back and turned towards the woman.

Rig stood and said, "The boy was merely curious is all."

The woman reached the boy, took his hand, and slapped it. "You don't talk to or touch strangers, do you understand me?" she barked.

The boy nodded.

Rig furrowed his brow at the strict mother and said, "The boy was only curious. It's not every day you see someone with a face like mine."

She leered at him and said to Joshua, "Stay away from strangers, you hear me."

As she pulled him away forcibly, Joshua waved to Rig.

Rig returned the wave then headed to the front desk. There he found Kyle with his head still down in the hotel ledger. "I need some information."

Kyle looked up. "Yes, sir." It took every bit of discipline to look upon Rig's face without showing the revulsion he was feeling in his body.

"I need to know where a town is," Rig said.

"What would the name be, sir?" Kyle asked.

"Mentryville, where is Mentryville?"

MENTRYVILLE, CALIFORNIA

James left his horse at home and decided to walk to his office. He often found walking helped him think more clearly than riding. As he strode along, taking in the sights of the bustling oil town, he became overwhelmed with a sense of dread. He had worked very hard since leaving Missouri, only to have it revisit him on the very day he was supposed to begin a new journey.

"Sir, you look like you need to repent your sins," a man called out from the side of the street.

James snapped out of his deep thoughts and gazed over to a man dressed in black with a white clerical collar around his neck, standing in front of a tent. Above the opening flap of the large tent was a handwritten sign, which simply read "CHURCH."

Locking eyes with James, the preacher said, "I see you and so does God. Come, friend, come and repent the sins that are burdening you."

James stopped and stared in awe at the odd timing of the interaction.

"Come, my friend, unburden yourself of these sins once and for all, and I promise you that God will deliver you," the pastor said.

Frozen to the spot, James pondered the time following the incident in Missouri and knew that while he had fled the consequences of his actions, he hadn't asked for forgiveness from God himself. Why was that?

The pastor left his station at the front of his tent and marched over to James. He put out his hand and said, "Bernard Jackson. I'm the minister of this church. I know it doesn't look like much, but God doesn't need a building made of wood or stone. He's present everywhere."

Taking his hand, James said, "I'm James Harris."

"Nice to meet you, brother James. Please step into my church and let go of your sins," Bernard said, motioning with his hand towards the tent.

As if being led by an invisible force, James began to walk towards the tent, only stopping just before he went inside.

Bernard opened the flap and said, "Please come in. I promise you that upon your exiting, you will be a different man."

James was unsure what he should do. In some ways he felt foolish, but then again what could it hurt to try? Taking a leap of faith, he entered the tent.

Bernard followed him in and closed the flap. "Take a seat."

James saw two small folding wooden chairs. He went to one and sat down.

Taking the seat opposite him, Bernard said, "I can tell by your attire and demeanor that you're a businessman. With that in mind, I'll be pithy. I'll say a prayer, and then when you're ready, you are welcome to unburden yourself."

"You expect me to tell you my sins?" James asked.

"You can have confidence that what you say here will not go beyond this meager canvas tent," Bernard said.

"How do I know this?" James asked skeptically.

"Because I'm a man of God, and knowing your sins doesn't provide me value; I gain nothing from that," Bernard answered.

James thought for a moment and said, "Go ahead, begin."

Bernard lowered his head and started to pray out loud.

James only slightly lowered his head so he could keep his eyes on Bernard. He watched him as he recited a prayer, which James thought sounded rehearsed. "Stop."

Bernard looked up and asked, "What is wrong?"

"This is a mistake," James said, standing up.

"I can assure you that you're supposed to be here. Why did you stop when I called out? Why are you here? You have something you want God to absolve you of, and I can help with that."

"This seems like an act. What's next, you'll ask me for a donation or you'll try to sell me some prayer beads or snake oil?" James asked sarcastically.

"I don't ask for donations, I don't sell anything, and I don't have snake oil, whatever that might be," Bernard said defensively. "Please, James, sit down. I'll skip the prayer."

"But why do I need to say it in front of you?" James asked.

"James, I can hear in your voice that you're in crisis. I'm here to tell you that God loves you and will forgive; what you must do is ask for his grace. You must confess and then do whatever else is necessary through action to receive redemption."

"So praying isn't enough?" James asked.

"No, you must also follow up by acting. You can't just commit sins then pray, only to go right back out and commit them again. Prayer isn't the only way; you must also strive to live a holy life."

James sat down again and said without hesitation, "At the end of the war, I took part in an attack that resulted in the death of innocent people. I fled my home state and came west. I'm now being threatened that this secret will be exposed. I fear my past has come back to haunt me because I never truly owned up to it. I never took responsibility for my foolish actions."

Bernard sat and watched, his facial expression stoic.

James continued, "I want God to know that I'm truly sorry. I didn't mean for that to happen. I thought what I was doing was just, that seeking revenge for my father's death gave me the justification to take others' lives. I've now come to discover that an eye for an eye is not the right path. I've strived very hard to live a good life, I provide for my family, I'm a good husband and father and only seek to be a greater person. I just don't know what to do right now. Two men from my past have shown up and mean to destroy the life I've created. On one hand I think I should take my family and run away, but on the other, I think I should stand my ground. I'm not the man I was eleven years ago; I'm different. I've never raised a hand against another in violence since and have sworn to never do it again. Do you see my confusion? If I get God's forgiveness, does that mean this will all go away?"

"I'm sorry to say that it won't. You did what you did, but you must still face the worldly consequences of that action. What you're doing by being here and seeking forgiveness from God is ensuring your place in the afterlife in heaven."

"But I need to make this right," James snapped in a show of his frustration as he got up and began to walk from one side of the tent to the other.

"James, you must bare your soul to God and then let things happen. Only then will you be absolved of your sins and be able to move forward. And remember this, we're talking about your eternal soul here," Bernard said.

James paced around the tent, stopping at a framed

drawing of Jesus Christ. He looked at the delicately drawn image and suddenly wondered, "Is this what he truly looked like?"

"Excuse me?" Bernard asked, unsure what James was talking about.

Stepping aside, James pointed at the drawing and asked, "This drawing of Jesus, is that what he looked like?"

"It's hard to know. I would say it's an inspired image of our Lord and Savior," Bernard answered with a slickness a politician would be proud of.

"How do I do this?" James asked.

"Are you talking about asking for forgiveness and confessing your sins?" Bernard asked.

"Yes," James replied.

"Get on your knees in front of the altar there, clasp your hands together, and declare to God your sins. Be honest; be sincere and contrite. You may lie to me, but God knows what's in your heart," Bernard said.

James rushed to the altar and dropped to his knees. He interlaced his fingers and began to run through the sins he was most concerned about.

Bernard stood back and watched without uttering a word.

When he was done, James stood. He felt a tear on his cheek and quickly wiped it away.

Bernard approached him from behind, placed a hand on his shoulder, and asked, "How do you feel?"

"To be honest, I feel good," James said.

"Good," Bernard said.

James removed his pocket watch and opened it to find

he'd been in the tent with Bernard for over thirty minutes. "I have to go," he said, moving towards the door.

Bernard followed.

Tossing the flap open, James went to exit but stopped short. He turned and said, "Thank you."

"I've done nothing, I merely gave you a place and some encouraging words; you did all the heavy lifting. Now go in peace, my friend, and, James?" Bernard said.

"Yes."

"Please come back and visit anytime. I am here to listen, give advice or just be a friend, because we all need friends now and then," Bernard said.

James nodded and exited the dimly lit tent into the bright late morning. He squinted from the sun's light, put on his hat, and headed to his office.

CHAPTER FOUR

SEPTEMBER 25, 1876

MENTRYVILLE, CALIFORNIA

Unable to sleep, James lay in bed and contemplated the next encounter he knew was coming with John and Cecil. He thought about bribing them, but what good would that do if he gave them money and didn't have an arrangement they'd abide by? He had no leverage on them, no means of stopping them. He was stuck with his only recourse being to just come clean with Emma and his partners.

The more he thought about telling Emma the truth, the more he grew concerned. She was the only person he was worried about taking his confession and using it against him. Not because she had a history of doing that, but because losing her was the one thing that would hurt him more than losing money or property.

"I can hear you thinking," she said.

Startled that she too was awake, he rolled onto his side and asked, "Did I wake you?"

"No, but I know when something is bothering you. I woke a little bit ago, and I could tell by your breathing that you were awake as well," she replied.

"You should go back to sleep," he said.

"James, what is wrong? And don't tell me it's the land deal; I know something is plaguing your thoughts."

"It's nothing," he replied.

"Even Scarlet knows," she said.

"She told you something?" he asked, scared that she had given away their secret.

"No, she didn't tell me anything. I heard her praying when I came home. She was asking God to watch over you and to protect you from two bad men," Emma said. She reached and turned up the lantern on her nightstand.

An orange glow illuminated the room.

She rolled onto her side and looked at him. "Who are these two men?"

Knowing that he couldn't lie anymore, he decided to open up completely and let the chips fall where they may. He sighed and asked, "Can you listen without judgment?"

"Of course," she answered.

"You know I'm from Missouri, but you never knew why I left. Well, it's because I did something very bad," he said, then paused to think about how he'd explain that night.

"Bad, like how bad?" she asked.

"I know I told you that my father was killed during the war. Well, all I ever wanted to do was avenge his death but didn't get my chance until just after the war ended. You see, in Missouri there were bands of guerilla fighters still waging war. I joined one of those groups; they went by the name Kemp's Raiders. What I didn't know was they weren't really fighting for the Confederacy, they were just riding the countryside, killing without regard, and looting whomever they came across," he said before pausing. He sighed and continued, "They took me in without question. I felt like I was now a part of something, that I had a purpose. Then that night came; it was May 17. I know it because that night changed my life. We had taken up position on the edge of a field near a small cabin that we were told was being used by Yankee soldiers. Being that it was my first battle with the Raiders, I was to initiate the attack. They sent me across the field with two torches. I was to throw them through the window and set the cabin ablaze to draw the Yankees out. Once they were outside, we'd gun them down." Again he stopped.

Seeing that he was getting emotional, she reached out and touched his hand.

"I approached the cabin window, and just as I was about to throw the first torch in, I saw women and children inside. I froze instantly, not sure what to do. My eyes darted around the small space, but nowhere did I spy a man in uniform, nothing like it. Men from the Raiders began to holler at me to toss the torch, but I couldn't. Then one of the children, a boy, saw me. We both locked our gazes upon the other. Cecil yelled at me to throw the torches, yet I couldn't. I looked at that boy and knew if I threw the torch, I'd be killing him. Then panic set in. If I didn't throw the torches, the Raiders would no doubt gun me down and possibly my mother. I was torn. Damned if I did and damned if I didn't. So like a coward I threw the torch in to save my own skin, but I didn't stop there. I hurled the second one in as well. And like a coward, I ran to take cover and watched in horror as the women and children fled the cabin, flames engulfing their bodies as the Raiders gunned them down."

Tears flowed from Emma's eyes as she listened to his story.

"I killed them, me, your husband, the man you came to love, caused the death of innocent women and children, and all because I valued my life more than theirs, and for what? Because I had a blood debt that I thought needed to be paid. I thought if I killed Yankees that somehow I would be getting the revenge I thought was necessary for my father. I was wrong, so wrong. I confronted Cecil and John Kemp, the leader of the Raiders, and told them what they had me do was not just wrong but amounted to murder. How could they claim what they were doing was war when they slaughter innocents? This wasn't war; there was no honor in what I did or what they were doing. I tossed my pistols down and walked away," he said, his eyes wet with tears.

"You've been carrying that around for all that time?" she asked.

"Yes, I'm sorry I never told you. I'm sure you think poorly of me now," he said.

"No, I don't. You were a young foolish boy who had his head filled with false stories. I'm not happy it happened, I'm sad for those people, but I know you're not that man now. You're not a killer. You were an innocent boy yourself, put in an untenable situation."

"You forgive me?" he asked.

"Forgive? There's nothing for me to forgive," she replied.

"I lied," he said.

"When did you lie to me? You just never told me it happened," she countered.

"But some consider an omission a lie," he said, seeking clarification.

"I could see where that makes sense in certain situations, but not this one unless you have more to tell and you're not," she said.

"There's more to tell," he confessed.

"I'm listening," she said.

"What you heard Scarlet praying about concerns two men who have come to town. These men are the very ones who bought that land out from underneath me. They went to Mr. Garcia and told him I was a murderer. They then showed up at the house yesterday morning while you were gone and threatened me. Scarlet overheard our conversation and came downstairs. She saw them…"

"Should I be worried?" she asked.

He thought for a moment about how he should respond and quickly decided to keep being honest. "We should be worried. These men are the very ones who had me throw those torches into that cabin eleven years ago. It's John Kemp and Cecil Brangan."

"Why are they here? What happened was so long

ago; you did nothing to them," she said.

"Apparently they were arrested after the cabin fire and placed in jail for nine years. They told me when they were here that they're here to take everything away from me," he said.

"What does that mean? Are they going to kill you?" she asked, her voice cracking.

"No, I don't believe so; otherwise I would have already been killed. I don't know how they knew where I was, but they showed up three weeks ago, inquired about the land we were negotiating on, and eventually stole it out from underneath us by spreading lies. Now I can only assume they intend to undermine my business or, worse, damage my reputation in town."

"We should leave…immediately," she snapped.

"No, we can't. We've worked too hard for where we are now," he said.

"We must think of Scarlet, of our safety," she said fearfully.

"We can't run. They told me if I did, they'd only pursue me. I ran eleven years ago and my past has caught up with me. It's time I finally confront this head-on. I told you, and now I plan on telling Christopher and William the truth. I thought I needed to fear what happened, but I know deep down I didn't murder those people. What I did was regretful, stupid, and foolish, but it has taught me that I need to cherish all life, that violence doesn't solve issues. No more running, Emma. This is where I take my stand."

She pondered what he said then thoughtfully replied, "I love you, and I'll do what you think is best.

We're a family and we'll conquer this together as one."

He embraced her and said, "I love you. I'm sorry I didn't feel I could trust you to tell you about this years ago."

"It's fine, but no more secrets," she said.

"I promise, but I should tell you that I told Scarlet not to tell you about the men being here."

"You did?"

"I was acting from fear. Please know that is the only secret I have," James said.

"Good, all is forgiven," she said.

"Thank you."

"Now tell me, how are we going to beat these men?"

***

Sitting in their hotel room, John kicked his legs up on the dresser while Cecil sat enjoying a freshly packed pipe.

"How long are we going to stay here?" Cecil asked.

"Why leave?" John replied with his own question.

"Because this is a small shit town, that's why. Let's head back to Dodge or even head to Deadwood; I've heard great things. We could get into gold mining."

"You know what, Cecil, those towns are no different than this one except that we have a real opportunity here. We could be more here. We came with the goal of getting retribution against James, but we may have found something bigger."

"You really want to get in the oil business? Who's

going to use oil? What's it all for? Now gold makes sense, oil doesn't," Cecil said.

"You heard what that Mexican fella told us when we inquired weeks ago. That parcel, which we now own, is rich with it. Look at how James reacted when we took it from him. We could be oilmen. This could be the place we set up shop and make a name and riches for ourselves."

"So you're telling me we're not leaving," Cecil lamented as he exhaled a cloud of smoke.

"No, we're not leaving. In fact, we're going to grow our footprint here. We're going to take over this town."

"And how do you suppose we do that? We're ex-convicts, outlaws; all of the money we've gotten has been through ill means," Cecil said.

"It's time we change that. It's time we leave our pasts. I have to respect James for what he's done. He left Missouri and came west; now he's doing good for himself. Thing is, we could do better because we don't have his morals to get in our way. We can take what we want. The small-minded folk around here won't see it coming," John said as his mind envisioned the town with his name on it.

"If we're going to stay, can we get better accommodations?" Cecil complained.

Laughing heartily, John said, "This room is luxurious compared to our little cell, but yes, we can find ourselves a proper house for you."

"Good."

John mused and said, "Kempville, that has a nice ring to it."

"How about Kemp Town?" Cecil shot back.

"I like it," John said, smiling, his arms crossed over his chest.

"Or we could call it Cecilville," Cecil joked.

"We can call the next town we take over after you, deal?" John asked sincerely.

"You mean that?" Cecil asked, shocked by the concession.

"I mean it. You've been loyal to me since the war, and I'll repay you for that loyalty, but first let's secure this town as ours. How much money do we have left over from the bank heist?" John asked, referring to a bank robbery the two had committed in Kansas upon their being released from prison.

"One thousand two hundred and sixty-seven dollars," Cecil answered.

John craned his head over to Cecil and said, "That's why I like and trust you, Cecil. You know the number down to the dollar."

"I can give it down to the cents if you want," Cecil quipped.

"Say, where's our food?"

"I'll go check," Cecil said, hopping up from his seat and rushing towards the door.

"Listen, after we eat, I want you to go set up a meeting with the old Mexican fella. If we're going to take over the town, it'll be a lot easier if we own it."

"I'll do that right away," Cecil said, opening the door.

Before he could leave, John had one other request. "And one more thing."

"What's that?" Cecil asked, his pipe dangling from his mouth.

"Any word on when our boys will be here?" John asked.

"John, if I knew, you'd know," Cecil said, referring to John's request to assemble as many men from the old Raiders as Cecil could find. He'd sent telegrams within days of their arrival weeks ago with hopes for them to gather and come to California.

"I need them here."

"Really?" Cecil asked, shocked by the request.

"If we're going to run a town, we'll need guns and muscle, you know this. Did you promise them riches beyond their wildest dreams?"

"I did, but what happens if they come and we don't have that sort of money?" Cecil asked.

"Don't worry about that, let me figure it out. I just want the boys assembled. It's time for the Raiders to ride again."

"I'll stop by the telegraph office and see if anything has come in."

"Wait, there is one more little thing that I need you to do, and you'll enjoy this," John said.

"What's that?"

"Go out to the bars and saloons, start spreading the word about our friend James, mention that he's unable to pay his people, that he's in financial trouble. Let's cause him a bit of heartburn."

"You're right, I'll enjoy that," Cecil said, taking a puff on his pipe.

"I knew you would. Now go, hurry, I'm hungry."

***

After James left to go to work, Emma went to Scarlet's room to talk about the situation facing their family.

"Scarlet, I need to talk to you," Emma said.

Taking a seat on her bed, Scarlet folded her hands and placed them on her lap. "Yeah, Mama, what is it?"

"The other day, two men came to the house…and you should know Papa told me, so you don't have to protect him."

"Yes, two men came. Bad men, I think."

"Yes, they're bad men. Your father and I spoke, and we're going to need to be more careful for the time being. Now I don't believe these men are here to hurt you or me, but we can't be too sure. What that means is we're going to go about our day differently than normal. I'm keeping you home from school and I'll not be going to my knitting group. I know you don't like that, as you love school, but until we know without a doubt that everything is okay, we need to be cautious," Emma said directly.

"Is Papa safe?"

"He should be, but he's also doing things differently."

"I'll keep praying. I've been doing it several times a day," Scarlet said.

"I heard you yesterday."

"Yes, I keep asking God to protect us, to send us someone to watch over us and keep Papa and us safe. A guardian angel, that's what I've been asking God for."

"Good, you keep praying, but more importantly, stay indoors, and don't answer the door if someone knocks," Emma ordered, stressing the practical response over the spiritual.

"Okay, Mama."

"You don't seem scared," Emma said, noticing Scarlet's nonchalant demeanor.

"It's because I know that our guardian angel is coming to protect us," Scarlet said confidently.

"Good, I'm sure they're coming, but like I said, until we know more, we'll just do things differently."

"Okay, Mama."

"Now come downstairs and help me prepare dinner for later. If you're not going to be in school, I'll at least teach you what I know in the kitchen," Emma said, standing up.

Scarlet hopped off the bed and said, "Don't worry, Mama, everything will be fine. I just know it."

"And how do you know that?"

"Because I keep praying. I know God will hear my prayers," Scarlet replied innocently.

Not wishing to diminish her spirit, Emma simply said, "You keep saying your prayers, and please, whatever you do, keep your faith. You never know when God answers prayers."

"He will, Mama, I just know it."

Emma embraced Scarlet and said, "I love you, little one, you have the biggest heart."

"I love you too, Mama."

"How about we read?"

"Okay," Scarlet said.

The two grabbed a book and cuddled on the bed.

CHAPTER FIVE

SEPTEMBER 26, 1876

MENTRYVILLE, CALIFORNIA

B anging on the front door woke James from a dead sleep. He sat up and listened, his heart racing.

"Do you think it's them?" Emma asked, her voice trembling.

"Mama, Papa," Scarlet whimpered as she ran into the room and hopped in the bed, her confident demeanor from the other day gone. She curled up in Emma's arms and asked, "Papa, are they here to hurt us?"

"Let me go see who it is," James said, tossing off the covers and racing towards the bedroom door.

"James, are you sure that's a good idea?" Emma asked.

"I don't think it's them. If they were coming to hurt us, they wouldn't knock, they'd just kick in the door," James replied before turning back and heading out the door. He sprinted down the stairs and into the foyer. "Who's there?"

"It's William. Open up."

"Are you alone?" James asked.

"Yes, I'm alone. Now open up the door; something has happened," William hollered.

James unlocked his door and opened it to find William standing on the porch lit by the light of the full moon. "What is it?"

"Can I come in?" William asked.

James looked over William's shoulder to make sure no one else was there.

Seeing what he was doing, William glanced around too before asking, "Are you expecting someone else?"

The aroma of alcohol then wafted over James. "You're drunk."

"I had a few drinks while playing poker. Now are you going to let me in or not?"

"Come in, hurry," James said, opening the door enough for William to walk in. Once inside, James closed the door and locked it. "What's so important?"

"Alejandro, the bastard, he sold all of his holdings, that includes all the buildings he owns in town, which also includes the office we lease."

"To whom?" James asked, although he suspected who it was.

"Those two men who bought our land, they secured it all," William said. His composure showed he was clearly rattled by the recent news.

Knowing he needed to be honest with William, as he had been with Emma, James said, "Come and take a seat in the parlor. There's something I need to tell you."

"Is something wrong?" William asked.

"Yes and no, it's best I explain it all from the beginning," James said, motioning for William to go to the parlor.

William heeded the call and took a seat in one of the wingback chairs. He was curious as to what James had to tell him.

"James, are you okay?" Emma called out from the top of the stairs.

James had forgotten about Emma and Scarlet. He went to the base of the stairs and replied, "It's William. He's got some interesting news about you-know-who. I'll tell you later."

"Okay," Emma said. "Scarlet is going to sleep in our bed."

"That's fine. I'll be up shortly," James said. He walked into the parlor to find William sitting in the dark. "Light a lantern. There's one next to you on a table to your right."

William lit the lantern and filled the room with a warm orange glow.

Taking the chair next to William, James said, "The two men who bought the land out from underneath us are old acquaintances of mine from Missouri."

"You know them?" William asked, shocked by the confession.

"Yes, I know them, but haven't seen them in eleven years. We fought in the same unit after the war ended."

"Please explain how you fought after the war," William said. Being from Montana territory, William and his family weren't partisans in the war, having remained in the seclusion of eastern Montana.

"We were with an outfit called Kemp's Raiders; we weren't regular army. We kept the fight going after the surrender," James explained.

"That's fine, but that doesn't explain why those men are here," William said.

"They're here to take vengeance on me for something I did. I had no idea they would take it this far."

"Vengeance for what?"

"Doesn't matter what. They're here now and it appears they're trying to take over the town," James said.

"We need to contact the sheriff, get him to come up here."

"To do what? Have they done anything illegal? We can't summon the sheriff based upon speculation. Alejandro may have decided to sell his entire stake in this area to those men, but what's the wrong in it as it pertains to the law? We don't know anything about these transactions," James said, trying to sound impartial although he felt something nefarious was at play.

"These men took our land because of a vendetta against you?" William asked.

"Correct," James confessed.

"When were you going to tell us?"

"Later today. I only found out yesterday; otherwise I would have told you sooner," James lied.

"If they now own the building we're leasing, we should expect an eviction notice any day."

"There's a good chance of that," James said. "Can you think of any other space we can lease?"

"No, on account that Alejandro pretty much owned

all the buildings in town. You do recall his family has been here for over a century," William snapped sarcastically.

"Listen, I know why you came here at this hour, but trust me, we will manage this situation, that's all we can do," James said, hoping to not only ease William's insecurities but his own.

"You're not upset about this?"

"I don't like it, but I need time to process," James replied. "I refuse to let my emotions or fear impact my decisions."

Agitated, William got to his feet and said, "I'll let you go back to sleep, and, James, next time you know something that affects me, please give me the courtesy of informing me."

"I was going to," James lied.

"I hope so," William said, his tone accusatory.

Not wanting to get into a back-and-forth with him, James stood and said, "Have a good night, and thank you for letting me know about what's happened. How about we meet tomorrow with Christopher and make a contingency plan?"

"Fair enough, I'll get word to him," William said then left the house.

James extinguished the lantern, locked the front door, and went back upstairs to find Scarlet sleeping soundly and Emma lying next to her wide awake.

"What did William want?" Emma asked.

James slid into bed. When his head hit the pillow, he answered, "Mr. Garcia sold his remaining assets to John and Cecil."

"What does that mean?" Emma asked, her voice just above a whisper.

"It means that our lives just got a bit harder," James answered.

CHAPTER SIX

SEPTEMBER 27, 1876

THREE MILES SOUTH OF MENTRYVILLE, CALIFORNIA

After another restless sleep, James could feel the fatigue and stress wearing on him. He'd never heard from William about a meeting and had even waited in the office for both to arrive, but neither did. Needing to be productive to ease his thoughts, he decided to go out to his well and oversee the operation.

When he arrived, he found half of his crew were off digging a second well about a quarter mile away. With all the flurry of recent activity, he'd forgotten about this new well dig. Eager to know the progress, he left directly for the new site.

The first thing he saw when he cleared the ridge was his men sitting around, not one working. He rode up and asked the foreman, a large burly man by the name of Aaron, "Why is everyone not working?"

Aaron jumped to his feet; he wiped his hands on his

denim pants. "Boss, we have a problem."

James dismounted and asked, "Well, what's the problem?"

"We've been digging and digging, but all we keep hitting is rock. The men are tired."

Knowing fatigue, James said, "So this is just a break?"

"Yes, boss."

James could sense that something else was bothering Aaron. "Walk with me," James said, tying his horse to a large bush.

The two walked to the hole that now spanned eight feet wide and twelve feet deep. James looked down and saw granite. "Is it a large boulder?"

"It's a good size, but we're working hard to bust it up. Once past it, we're hoping to put the drive pipe in and begin drilling down," Aaron said.

Familiar with the situation, as he had dealt with it when he dug his first well with his own hands, James removed his coat and tie and handed them to Aaron.

"What are you doing, boss?" Aaron asked.

"I'm going to work," James replied. "Where's the dynamite?"

"Boss, I only like to use that for situations that warrant it."

James looked down the hole. "That's a boulder, Aaron. Why are you trying to break it up? Just blow it out of there," James asked, confused by what was happening.

"On account…" Aaron said before pausing.

"Tell me."

"We don't have any," Aaron confessed as he lowered

his head in shame.

James could feel the anger rising. "What do you mean we don't have any. Go into town and get some."

"There isn't any. It's sold out. I tried," Aaron answered.

"Then go to my partners' operations; buy some from them."

"I did and they won't sell me any," Aaron said. "In fact, boss, that's the problem with the men. They've heard some stories…"

"Stories?"

"Yes, about you."

"Tell me," James ordered.

"As you know, the men tend to drink and spend time with others from different crews around these parts—"

Interrupting Aaron, James snapped, "Just spit it out."

"They heard that you might not be operating soon, that this here might shut down. Something about you being in a bit of trouble."

"I'm not in any trouble as it pertains to my operation. I had trouble acquiring that new plot, that's it, nothing else. Whatever the rumors are in town, they're wrong," James said defiantly.

"You see, boss, the men thought that too. Then when we tried to buy from your partners, of all people, they wouldn't deal with us," Aaron said.

Seeing how that could bolster the rumors, James decided to tell Aaron part of the story. "My partners are upset with me on account I didn't tell them fast enough about why we didn't get the plot. They're apparently holding it against me, but I can assure you…" James said before stopping and looking towards the huddled men nearby. "I'll address this with them directly." James marched to the crew.

All their eyes watched with anticipation as James approached.

Rolling up his sleeves, James stopped in front of the crew and said, "I know you've heard rumors. What I can tell you is that my operation, my first well and this well, is in good standing financially. What you've heard in town pertains to a failed acquisition of a plot of land, nothing more. My partners and I did not get that plot because of bad blood between me and the men who acquired it. If you're hearing that I don't have the money to keep this operation running or to pay you, etcetera, those are false. Behind me is the potential for another two barrels per day. We need to get this well drilled and producing."

"How do we know you're going to pay us?" a man called out.

"Don't ask the boss questions," Aaron barked.

Waving his hand to show it was fine, James said, "It's okay, they're concerned, I understand." He turned to the man and stared into his eyes. He knew what they were thinking, as he'd been there before. They had families to feed and needed the work. If they felt one bit uncomfortable about that prospect, they would all get up and leave. What he needed to do to ensure his operation didn't suffer from lack of men was to be bold. He quickly thought and came up with a plan. "Here's what I'm going to do to prove to you that we're fine financially. I'm going to have you paid at the end of every day of work."

Some of the men nodded their approval while others still weren't convinced.

James knew that wouldn't be enough to keep them coming back if other operations started up, which was highly probable with John and Cecil owning the new plot. "I'm going to offer you something that no other company anywhere would, and that is a share in the profit."

A few men gasped while others began to chatter among themselves.

"You heard that right. You're putting in your sweat equity, so I'll pay that by giving you a profit from this well. Each man in my crew will earn two cents per barrel of oil that comes out of any of my wells."

Some men cheered the news, but still there were doubters.

Knowing that he had more than likely secured the loyalty of enough to keep his operation humming, James said, "If you're with me, let's get this rock out of that hole and start drilling. The faster we can get the oil out of there, the faster you'll make that money."

Most of the men jumped to their feet and hurried towards the hole. Two men didn't.

"What's the issue?" James asked the two men.

"We're not sure you're telling us the truth," one of the men said.

James walked over, placed his hand on the man's shoulder, and said, "This deal is only good for now. If you walk, there's no coming back. You'll not get this deal anywhere else."

The two men looked at each other, then gave James a nod. "We're with you."

"Good, now get to work," James said. He felt a sense of relief wash over him. He knew he'd given up profit, but with oil at two dollars and fifty-six cents per barrel, he had some to spare. It was better to have a bit less profit than no profit at all.

"What are we going to do about that rock?" Aaron asked.

"Black powder."

Aaron's eyes lit up. "I'll send some men in now."

"No, you go, get ten pounds of black powder. We'll bust cracks in the rock while you're gone so we can pour the powder down," James said.

"Yes, boss," Aaron said and hurried off.

James walked over to his men. Several had gone down into the hole. Needing to physically show them that they were in this together, he went down into the hole and said, "Give me that."

The man handed him a pickax. "We're going to bust cracks in this. When Aaron returns with some black powder, we're going to fill the cracks and crevices with it and light it up. That should be enough to break this up so we can place the drive pipe."

The men nodded.

With the pickax firmly in his grip, James swung. When the iron head struck rock, he could feel it all the way through his body and loved it. He wasn't going to let anyone stop him. Even if it meant he would have to be back in the wells digging or working, this was his, and no one was going to take it away.

MENTRYVILLE, CALIFORNIA

Each time a hoof of his horse touched the ground, James felt the jolt going through his aching body. Having spent the entire day at well number two, he could say that the pain he was feeling was justified, as they'd managed to get the drive pipe in the ground and had begun drilling. Now all that needed to happen was to hit a pocket of oil.

The hard work and focus gave him a reprieve from the other issues in his life, specifically the strained relationship he apparently had now with his partners. He pondered now just how to deal with it but couldn't find an answer. So much for honesty, he thought. What struck him the most was Christopher's response. He clearly had been made aware, and one could only think that he'd sent word down to his crew not to support him. How else could he explain what had happened with Aaron when he went to secure some dynamite.

He pulled the reins on his horse gently to steer him towards his house when he spotted Christopher himself walking across the street.

Christopher had his head down and was in deep thought.

James couldn't think of a better time to talk than now. "Christopher!" he hollered.

Stunned to hear his name, Christopher looked up and around for the source. He spotted James, but instead of stopping or acknowledging him, he increased his pace.

"Christopher, stop, we need to talk!" James shouted.

James' call was loud enough to get passersby to glance his way.

"Chris, stop, damn it. We need to talk!" James again cried out.

Ignoring James, Christopher kept walking towards his destination, the local feed store.

Not one to be easily disregarded, James rode over and blocked Christopher's path. "We're going to talk, do you hear me?"

"I have nothing to say to you," Christopher bluntly shot back.

Finding his response unusual, James hopped from the horse quickly and got in Christopher's face. "Chris, it's me. We need to talk about what's going on."

"So you can lie to me?" Christopher asked.

"I've never lied to you," James said, defending himself.

"Will told me everything, and now I'm hearing other rumors. Why didn't you come to us if you didn't have the funds to continue our partnership?" Christopher asked.

"Funds? I'm not insolvent. I have more than we needed for my share. Hell, my third was already in the account at the bank. I'm not sure what you're talking about," James said, dismayed by the accusation.

"James, I like you, so what's transpired has hurt me. You know I'm not one to pass harsh judgments, but I need to look out for myself now. You may not have lied, but you misrepresented yourself. You're not the man I thought. I don't know what to believe, but Belinda is worried that being associated with you could damage beyond repair what I've built here."

"Please believe me that what you've heard about my being unable to pay is a lie, a fabrication. I don't know who is spreading that rumor, but I'm not in financial trouble. Think about it, these two men come into town, they want payback against me, so they buy that parcel out from underneath us, now they're going around spreading rumors. Please, Chris, I need friends, and I count you as one of my closest," James begged.

"Listen, James, I can't, not right now. Maybe when the storm blows over, we can work together again."

"That's not what friends do. If you're going to abandon me now, then don't come back later, because you're not to be trusted," James snapped.

"That's how I feel about you," Christopher said.

"But I didn't do anything. I didn't tell you about my past because what did it matter? I didn't do what some have said, and regardless, I'm not that man anymore. Please don't let them win," James urged.

Christopher could see the pain in James' eyes. He wanted to help, but he also had to answer to his new bride, who was terrified that hitching himself to James would damage what they had. "Sorry, James, I can't."

James lowered his head. "I'm sorry to hear that."

Patting him on the shoulder, Christopher said, "You take care of yourself."

"Yeah, sure."

"Oh, I forgot, we're dissolving the incorporation. You can pick up your share of the monies from that account tomorrow," Christopher said.

"You don't even consult me?" James asked.

"No, Will and I didn't. This is what it is. Like I said, when this blows over, maybe then we can talk," Christopher said.

Anger welled up inside James. He'd diverted one catastrophe today but couldn't avert this one. He clenched his fists and looked deeply into Christopher's blue eyes. "You walk away, our friendship ends. I pray you never need me in the future, because if you do, I won't be there."

"Sorry, James," Christopher said before he stepped around James and walked off.

James stood in the middle of the busy street, his head down.

Several men walked past him. One man said, "That's him, that's James Harris. I heard he's about to go bankrupt."

Overhearing the men, James shouted, "Lies, all lies."

The men craned their heads back and gave James a wary look.

"You've heard nothing but lies and slander. I'm not about to go bankrupt, and I'll prove it, you hear me, I'll prove it!" James blared as he watched the men walk off. Out of the corner of his eye, he spotted Cecil leaning up against a post watching him. Unable to control his anger, he took off in his direction.

Cecil removed the pipe from his mouth and shoved it into his pocket. He squared up and placed his right palm on the back strap of his Colt.

James came in like a wild man. "You! You and John

started these lies!"

"I don't know what you're talking about," Cecil replied with a snarky grin.

"You've been going around spreading lies that I'm going bankrupt or don't have the means to pay my men. That is a flat-out lie," James howled as he pointed at Cecil with a trembling hand.

"And if it were true, so what? What are you going to do about it? Nothing, am I right?" Cecil asked, mocking him.

"You leave me, my family and my business alone. You can do whatever you want in this town, just leave me out of it," James snapped.

The altercation had drawn a small crowd of onlookers, who stood a safe distance back and watched.

"Why don't you carry a gun?" Cecil asked.

"If I did, I'd gun you down right here and right now," James fired back.

"Would you now?" Cecil laughed. "Please go get yourself some irons and come back. I'll be waiting."

Knowing that this wasn't going anywhere and having satisfied his need to confront Cecil, James spat on the ground and said, "Just stop, you hear me?"

"And what will you do?" Cecil asked.

James' entire body began to shudder in anger. He swiftly turned around and marched back to his horse, which was lingering near the opposite side of the road.

"Where are you going? Come back and let's settle this like men," Cecil mocked.

James got to his horse, mounted it, and trotted off

down the street. He could hear Cecil continue to taunt him until he rounded the corner on the last street. What was he going to do? He had vowed to never act out in anger, but if he did nothing, he could very well lose everything. He felt lost and unsure of himself. Maybe he should abandon what he'd created there and go back to Tucson or somewhere new. He needed to act and fast.

YUMA, ARIZONA TERRITORY

Looking west, Rig could see the bend in the Colorado River. Beyond that stood Fort Yuma on the California side of the river. His destination though was the settlement of Yuma, which also housed the Yuma Quartermaster's depot and was a bevy of activity and commerce. There he'd find a place to rest for the night as well as get resupplied for the remaining part of his journey. He was unsure which trail to take, but he had no doubt he'd be able to get accurate information from the military or someone in town.

Hitching Fire to a post, he went directly into the tent aptly marked SUPPLIES. Inside, he experienced the typical stares and gawks he'd get anywhere. He gathered what he needed, some feed for Fire, hardtack, jerky, ammunition for his pistol, and a new flint. Making his way to the clerk, who sat at a long table, he was stopped by a woman.

She placed her hand on his chest and began to massage him. "You look like you're in need of some attention."

Taken aback by her approach, considering his face, he

said, "Everyone could use some attention."

"I'm not talking about everyone, I'm talking about you," she purred.

He guessed she was no more than nineteen and very attractive. He wondered what would make such a beautiful young woman turn to prostitution. "What happened to you?"

"I'm in here getting some things and saw you," she replied.

"No, what happened to you? Why are you doing this?"

"You look like someone who could use a woman's time."

"You still didn't answer my question, but let's skip that. You feel sorry for me?" he asked.

Touching his face, she said, "I do."

For a brief second he allowed her gentle touch on his face before pulling back.

"I won't hurt you, I promise," she said, moving her hand back down to his chest and rubbing.

"Damn it, Val, you can't be in here doing that! Go back to Sweeney's," the clerk yelped.

"Leave me be, Ed. This here man needs me," Val spat back.

"Actually, I—" Rig said before being interrupted as Val covered his mouth with her hand.

"That might be, but you know the marshal has set them rules—all whiskey and women at the far end of town, not in the market square," Ed barked.

Val snarled and said to Rig, "You go finish your business and meet me outside."

"But I—" he said and again was silenced.

Slapping him on his butt, she said, "Go, hurry, get your things and, big man, do you mind buying this for me?" She set what could only be described as a stack of small hand-size towels and a tin of petroleum jelly into his hands. She gave him a quick wink and rushed out of the tent.

Rig felt a warmth rush over his body. It had been a very long time since he'd had a woman touch him, much less give him an ounce of sensual attention. He stared in the direction she'd gone, unsure of what had just happened.

"You're another sucker." Ed laughed.

Breaking the daze he was in, Rig approached the table and set his items down, including hers.

Ed took her things and set them apart. "Sorry about that. She tries that a lot."

"Tries what?" Rig asked, clueless.

Laughing, Ed replied, "Oh my, she got you all worked up, didn't she."

"She's really nice," Rig said.

"She's a damn whore. They're all nice when they want something," Ed snarked. He counted out what Rig had and said, "Seven dollars."

Looking down, Rig saw her things weren't with his. "And those."

"Mister, she's only taking advantage of you, nothing more."

"I don't care. How much?"

Ed frowned and said, "You know what this stuff is for, don't you?" He held up the tin of petroleum jelly.

"I use it for my skin," Rig said, and it was true, he applied it to his scars.

"Yeah, she uses it for her skin too," Ed joked. "Seven dollars, please."

"No, how much for her things too?" Rig asked, insistent.

Ed sighed and answered, "A dollar fifteen."

Rig paid the man and gathered all the items in his arms. "Thank you."

"A damn fool is born every day," Ed said.

Anxious to see her again, Rig exited the tent and looked around for Val but didn't see her. He instantly became sad.

"Over here, darling." Val giggled.

Like a schoolboy with a crush, he raced over to her and said, "Here are your things."

She leaned in and gave him a peck on his scarred left cheek. "You are a sweet thing."

He blushed.

She took her things, turned and took a step but paused. Looking back, she asked, "Do you want to come with me?"

Rig nodded.

"Then come on, big boy," she said and sauntered off, her hips shaking.

MENTRYVILLE, CALIFORNIA

The sound of the crackling fireplace soothed James' frazzled nerves. His day had started many hours ago and had been one issue after another. As he sipped a glass of brandy, he wondered what tomorrow would bring.

Emma entered the parlor and joined him. She'd seen the tension in him the second he arrived but said nothing because she already knew what vexed him.

Knowing he needed to tell her, James opened up. "John and Cecil have spread rumors in town that my company is in financial trouble. They've gone as far as spreading falsehoods that I can't pay my men."

"Where did you hear this?" Emma asked.

"My men for one, and then I ran into Christopher. I had to physically block him so he'd speak to me," James said, putting the glass to his lips. He sipped and said, "It appears my partners have also turned against me. We needed some dynamite for the second well, and they wouldn't sell any to us; in fact, no one would."

"They're out to destroy you."

"They are and I need to figure out a way to stop them."

"No, I'm talking about William and Christopher," Emma said.

James craned his head and asked, "You think I need to worry about them as well?"

"I do. William has always rubbed me wrong. He's quick to anger, and clearly he's not loyal. And then there's Christopher. He's weak; he will go where there's least resistance."

James put his gaze back on the fire, its flames dancing and flickering. He watched and thought.

"Maybe we should leave, sell the operation and go

back to Tucson. My father will help us," Emma said.

Not having to think a second, James snapped, "No. I'm not leaving."

"You can't be so rigid on this. We're not quitting, we're simply doing what is expedient," Emma said. She had spent the day thinking about it and, after hearing what had happened today, was more galvanized to the idea of packing up and going back to Arizona.

"No, I left Missouri, and look what's happened. I won't leave all I've created here. I need to finally stand up to John and Cecil," James countered.

"You need to think of me and Scarlet."

"Then maybe you and she should leave, go back to Tucson until this is all over."

Stunned, she said, "We're a family, and we do things together. I'm not leaving you here."

"Then we all stay."

"James, please listen to reason."

He leaned over the arm of the chair and drew closer to her. "I'm being reasonable. Leaving won't solve this issue. They explicitly told me that they'd follow me anywhere. So going back to Tucson wouldn't end this, it would merely prolong it. Where would we go after that? How would your father like it if I tarnished your family name in his town?"

"Then what are we going to do?"

"I don't know yet," he answered honestly.

Needing to shift to something more innocent, Emma said, "I forgot to tell you, but the other day, Scarlet was so sweet. She said that a guardian angel is coming to help us."

He looked at her, his expression softer, and said, "She told me she's going to keep praying."

"That's what she said to me as well."

"Thank you."

Raising her brow, she asked, "For what?"

"For being an amazing mother. Scarlet is an incredible and thoughtful child; she's obedient and always there to help. I know she didn't learn that from me," James said tenderly as he reached for her hand.

Emma took it and said, "She's a gift from God, that's for sure. I don't think I can take credit."

"Maybe she's right."

"About what?"

"That we should let go and have faith that God will help us. I know I try but quickly revert back to thinking I can't just sit back and let this happen, that I need to take action. What's so troubling though is I don't know what action to take," James confessed.

"You'll find the right answer."

"Then again, maybe Scarlet is right and a guardian angel will appear and sweep all of our troubles away."

"I don't have the heart to tell her that guardian angels aren't real," Emma said.

"Blasphemy." He chuckled.

"You know me, I believe, I have faith, but an angel sent from God to help us? No, I don't think it's true."

"Maybe it's not, or maybe it is. I'd like to think it's real, sort of gives me hope," James said. His eyes widened when the memory of the other day popped in his head. "Something peculiar happened the other day. I was walking down the street to my office when a man, a pastor or preacher, called out to me. He wanted me to come pray in a tent, which he called his church." James paused and thought about the moment. "What's so odd is the man picked me out of the crowded street. He seemed to know I was struggling with something and that I had a sin that needed to be voiced."

"What did you do?"

"I went in the tent and prayed for God to forgive me for what happened back in Missouri. I opened my heart and actually prayed."

"Who was this preacher?" Emma asked. "I haven't seen any new church."

"It's not a church per se, just a tent. The man was about my age, maybe a few years older. His clothes were a bit ragged, and just above the flap of the tent was a handwritten sign that read CHURCH. Inside were several chairs and a small altar."

"Where was this?" Emma asked.

"Right on Main Street, a half block from my office."

"He's not there now."

"Maybe he moved. It was just a tent," James said, not thinking much about it.

"How did you feel after you prayed?"

"To be honest, I felt good. It did feel like a weight had been lifted."

"Good, glad you got something out of it," Emma said.

The two sat silent for a moment.

"I hope Scarlet is right and there is a guardian angel coming," James said as he tenderly squeezed Emma's hand.

"Me too."

"What's that verse in the Bible, 'Out of the mouth of babes and sucklings'?"

"I know it," Emma said.

"Maybe Scarlet knows something we don't, and our guardian angel is on his way."

YUMA, ARIZONA TERRITORY

A swift cool breeze blew open the flap of the tent and chilled Rig. He pulled up the blanket to cover him and Val, who lay asleep next to him.

She'd taken him back to where she lived, and the two had made love. When she removed her clothes, he then knew why she had been kind to him. It wasn't because she wanted him to buy her things, which, of course, she didn't mind him doing; it was because she too was covered in scars from a house fire. From the back of her shoulders down to her lower back, thick scars covered her skin. Unafraid to show herself, she stripped down and went to him. He had caressed her skin and found her absolutely beautiful. For the first time in his life he had a real connection with someone.

As he lay there, he touched her skin once more, tracing the lines of each scar with his index finger.

His touch woke her.

"Well, hello," she purred.

"Hi."

"How old were you?" she asked, sitting up.

"Huh?"

"Your burns, how old were you when you were burned?" she asked.

"Young, elevento be exact."

"I was twelve."

"How did it happen?" he asked.

"A house fire started by my father. He had heard that I kissed a boy, a neighbor, and commenced beating me. In the tussle, he knocked over a lantern, and some of the oil spilled onto the back of my dress. I went up in flames immediately. He managed to put it out but not before it did what you see," she explained.

"He beat you?"

"I would've taken the beating over the burns, but I didn't have a choice."

"I'm sorry that happened to you," he said.

"I'm sorry too. After I healed, I ran away. I haven't seen him or my mother in six years."

"And now you're in Arizona…" he said, pausing.

"Yes, I'm a prostitute. I can't get work anywhere else and I need the money. Men also don't want someone who is damaged goods."

"What?"

Laughing, she said, "If anyone should know how people treat you when you're scarred, it's you."

"But it's my face," he said, challenging her.

"I was engaged once. When we were getting a little familiar, my fiancé discovered my secret; the next day the engagement was off. That was two years ago; he up and left town in the middle of the night."

"I don't understand. Your face is so beautiful; you don't look like a gruesome monster like me. He's a fool," Rig said defiantly.

"He is a fool, and you're not a gruesome monster," she said, taking his face in her left hand and bringing it towards hers. She kissed him and said, "You're handsome, and I can tell by your eyes that you're a good man."

Never in his life had he felt this way. It had come on so suddenly that it didn't make sense. He had met her only a couple of hours ago, yet he had feelings of love. He quickly dismissed them as immature notions from a man who had hardly any experience with women.

"Can I ask you a personal question?" she asked.

"Yes, you can."

"How many women have you been with?"

"A few," he lied.

"You can tell me," she said. "I won't judge you."

"Two, including you," he confessed. "Was it noticeable?"

"A bit, you were very earnest. I think your hands touched me everywhere." She giggled.

"I apologize," he said sheepishly.

"No, no, please don't say that. I quite enjoyed it. I didn't feel like a piece of meat to you, so thank you."

A head popped into the tent. "Valerie Mae, what are you doing?" a young woman asked.

Feeling embarrassed, Rig turned his face so that the scarred side was not facing the woman.

"I'm with a friend," Val replied.

"He looks handsome," the woman purred.

"If you can give us some privacy, we're not done yet," Val said.

"Well, when you're done, Grant is looking for you. He said he has an appointment with you," the woman said.

"Okay, I'll be there soon," Val said.

The woman left as quickly as she had come.

"Who's Grant?" Rig asked although he knew the answer.

"A customer," she answered without shame.

"Do you need to go?" Rig asked.

"Not yet, I'm quite enjoying our time together."

The two continued to talk and get to know each other, both losing track of time.

The flap of the tent again flew open, but this time it wasn't the woman but Grant himself. "There you are."

Both were surprised by the visit with Val shouting, "Grant, I told Hillary I'd come see you as soon as I was done with this gentleman. Now go away."

"No, you said four and it's now four forty-five. You're late; it's my time," Grant snapped. He was fully inside the tent, his arms folded in anger.

"Grant, get the hell out of here," Val fired back.

"No, we had a prearranged appointment," Grant said.

"The lady said to go away," Rig said calmly.

Grant cocked his head and gave Rig an annoyed look. "Listen here, freak, I pay good money for her every week, and now it's my time."

Sitting up more, his spine growing, Rig said, "I suggest you leave, now."

"I'm not leaving. This whore is now mine. Pack your

trash, freak, and go join a circus."

Rig threw the sheet off him and stood. Even naked, his presence was towering and impressive. "I'll give you one more chance or I'll hurt you."

Grant pulled his suit coat back to reveal a holstered pistol. "You're not going to hurt anyone."

Rig didn't think another second about what he did next. He leapt for Grant and grabbed him before he could draw his pistol. He head-butted him, shattering Grant's nose, then wrapped his large hands around his neck and pushed him out of the tent.

Grant toppled to the ground hard. As he lay there, he cried out in pain.

Rig exited the tent, paying no regard to his current state of dress. With both hands he picked Grant up off the ground, cocked his right arm back, and drove his fist into his face.

The punch landed squarely on Grant's chin, both knocking him out and breaking his jaw.

Grant's body went limp.

Rig threw him onto the ground, disarmed him, and went back inside the tent. Looking at Val, he said, "He won't be bothering you anymore."

"Damn it, he's a good customer, always pays good," Val complained.

"Whatever he pays you, I'll pay double. In fact, I'll do that for all your customers," Rig declared.

Her anger turned to empathy. "I don't know you, but that has to be the most romantic thing anyone has ever said to me."

"I want you to come with me if you want," Rig offered.

"Come with you? Where are you going?"

"California," he answered.

"I don't know you. Heck, I don't even know your name," she said.

Being as proper as he could muster considering he was naked, he reached out with his open hand and said, "My name is Rig. Pleasure to meet you."

She took his hand and, with a perplexed look, said, "Hi, Rig."

"Now you know my name and we obviously know each other," he said, clearing his throat. "So come with me; stop this work. I'll take care of you now."

She got up from the bed, walked over to him, and wrapped her arms around him. "I don't know who you are, but you're something else. However, if I ran off with every man who has wanted to rescue me, I would have traveled around the world a hundred times over."

"I'm not every other man, I'm me."

"Oh, sweetie, I can't run off with you. I work here. I don't know you; this will never work."

"You want to stay and be a prostitute?" he asked, confused by her refusal.

"No, I don't want to be a prostitute, but how do I know you won't get bored with me and just leave me when you're done with me?"

"Because I won't."

"But I don't know that."

"I swear to you and God that I would never abandon

you," he professed.

She shook her head, kissed his cheek, and said, "My place is here."

"No, it's not. Come with me. I'll buy you a house; we'll settle down."

She pulled away and said, "You're like a little boy in some ways. It's adorable, but I need a man who I know truly loves me, not just lusts after me or wants me because I gave them the time of day."

Stung by her comments, he lowered his head and began to doubt everything he'd just done.

"You see, you're already questioning everything," she said.

"Only because you're so insistent that it won't work. I can assure you that you'll be safe with me. I have money; you won't want for anything."

"How long are you going to California for?"

"Not sure, a few days or a few weeks, all depends," he replied.

"How about this? When you're done with what you're doing in California, if you still feel this way about me, come back, then I'll seriously consider your offer."

"You'll only consider it if I return?"

"Aren't you a stickler for words? I'll go with you if you return and still want me," she said.

He stuck out his hand and said, "Let's shake on it."

Chuckling, she said, "We're making a deal?"

"Yes."

She took his hand and shook. "It's a deal, then."

"Can you make me one other promise though?"

"And that is?"

"You don't work. I'll pay you what money you need; just be here when I return," he said, walking over to his gear. He opened the flap of his saddlebag, removed a pouch, and took out a handful of coins. "How much?"

Shocked by the amount of money he had on him, she said, "I can't take your money."

"How much to have you not work? Give me a price."

"Two hundred," she replied, just tossing out a number.

He counted out that amount and handed it to her. "There, two hundred."

Looking at the money in her hands, she said, "You're serious?"

"I am."

"Then I'll be seeing you when you return," Val said. "Now that it appears my schedule is open, how about we jump back in bed?"

A crooked smile stretched across his face. He took her by the hand and led her back to the bed.

CHAPTER SEVEN

SEPTEMBER 28, 1876

MENTRYVILLE, CALIFORNIA

U nsure what his day would be like, James just assumed that there would no doubt be obstacles. As he passed the office he shared with William and Christopher on his way to well number two, he decided to stop by and talk to them.

William spotted James coming and got Christopher's attention. The two exited the office and stood on the walkway.

"Good day, James," William said, leaning up against a post.

Tipping his hat, James said, "Good day, William. I see you can still access the office." He remained tall in his saddle.

"We can, but I fear you'll have to vacate," William said.

"And why is that?" James asked, his tone sounding annoyed.

"On account that was the arrangement I made with your old acquaintance John Kemp," William said.

"Just like that you discard me. I suppose it's better I learn now than have to suffer if we were partners on a parcel," James seethed.

"I feel the same way," William said.

"What was the point of coming to my house the other night? You wanted my guidance; then the second you see that I'm a bit vulnerable, you decide to cut me loose," James snapped.

"You lied to us, Jim, lied! And look at what you did, you killed women and children," William crowed.

James sighed loudly. The last thing he wanted to do was get into a back-and-forth with a man who had the immaturity of a teenaged boy.

Stepping out further, Christopher said, "Morning."

"Hi, Christopher," James replied.

"How about you come around later today or tomorrow to get your things?" Christopher said.

"I can stop by at the end of the day," James said. "Will my key work?"

"No, we're—" William said but was cut off.

Interrupting William, Christopher said, "Yes, just come by then." He shot William a hard look and said, "Stop badgering him."

"He's a liar. You heard what Kemp said," William barked.

"The only liars are him and his cohort Cecil. They're murderers, thieves, you name it, and now you're in bed with them," James said.

"I only see one liar here," William said.

"I can't believe for the life of me that you turned so quickly. I've had you at my dinner table, we've broken bread together, and in an instant you turn tail and run away from me."

"Like Alejandro, I don't do business with liars and killers," William said.

"You speak about things you know nothing about, Will; I feel for you, I do," James said, feeling his anger well up inside.

"How about you go. I fear this isn't productive for anyone," Christopher said.

"I agree," James said, again tipping his hat but this time to Christopher. "Thank you for your kindness."

"I'm sorry it's worked out this way," Christopher said.

"I am too," James said. He shot a look to William, but instead of saying anything, he clenched his teeth tightly.

"Try not to kill anyone today," William snarled.

James shook his head in disbelief. He had always known William was short-tempered and could be sharp tongued, but the treatment he was receiving from him was beyond the pale for anyone living in civilized society.

"You need to treat him with greater respect. Just days ago we called each other friends and partners," Christopher scolded William.

"I don't see you doing business with him anymore," William fired back.

"That's different than disrespecting the man and calling him names like a child," Christopher barked.

"I don't need you to tell me how to act," William said

and walked back in his office.

Christopher watched as James trotted away and genuinely felt for his old partner. He didn't like having to abandon him like he did, but he felt powerless.

With any sense of decorum gone between him and William, James pushed aside any thoughts of ever reconciling with his old partners if he was to ever clear his name. In some ways there was a sense of certainty in the way they acted towards him. He knew exactly who his friends were and weren't.

James then thought of the preacher and pulled back on the reins. His horse stopped. He craned his head back and looked down the street from which he came, but like Emma said, the tent wasn't there. "Where did you go?"

YUMA, ARIZONA TERRITORY

With Fire loaded up and ready for the ride to California, Rig walked to Val to say goodbye.

"I never did ask how long I have to wait," Val said.

"Three weeks, and if I don't return then, go about your life," Rig said.

"Three weeks it is, then," she said, putting her arms around him.

Feelings of insecurity washed over him suddenly. "I know I was forceful in my demands of you being with me, but I only want you if you want me."

"Do I want to live this life any longer? No. Do I know what my life will be with you? No. But could my life with you have potential? Yes. Does living here, doing what I'm doing, have potential? No. So you see, I have to go with the one yes."

"And this doesn't bother you?" he asked, motioning towards his face.

"Not at all," she replied.

"Are you sure?"

Pulling back from his embrace, she asked, "Where is the man I met who was sure of himself yesterday? The man who broke Grant Johnson's jaw and stole my heart?"

"He's here," Rig proclaimed. "I stole your heart?"

"You did. I don't know how you did it, but maybe it's your gentle eyes or the way you were with me."

"I'll take care of you," he said, again stressing his pledge to her.

"What's odd is I believe you. That's not like me. I don't trust men, so you'd be the first one; so that says something right there."

"And you'll wait?" he asked, once more showing his insecurity.

"I said I would. We made a deal, remember?"

"Okay."

"You never told me what you do. Why are you going to California?" she asked.

He thought about how he could describe to her what exactly he did. It wasn't a job, so to speak, and money always seem to be available to him when he needed it. How could he explain it to her?

"Do you not wish to tell me?"

"It's not that," he said.

"Are you a bounty hunter or gunslinger?" she asked,

her tone sounding aroused by the possibility of him being a gunman or something similar.

"You could say I'm an administer of justice."

"You're a lawman? Like a marshal?"

"Yeah, a lawman," he replied.

"That must be why I feel safe around you," she said, pulling him closer and draping her arms over his broad shoulders again.

He had an urge to say he loved her, but thought it was premature for such pronouncements. Holding her tight, he said, "I'll return soon."

"I'll be waiting."

He pulled away, leapt onto Fire's back, and took the reins in his grasp. "'Til then."

She blew him a kiss and said, "Until we see each other again."

MENTRYVILLE, CALIFORNIA

Cecil burst through the door of an office space they had just leased and shouted, "They're here. The boys are here!"

John grinned and slowly stood up from behind his large wooden desk. He donned his wide-brimmed hat and strutted to the door. "How many came?"

"All of them," Cecil said with a twinkle in his eye.

John put both hands on Cecil's narrow shoulders and said, "Good job, Cecil, good job."

"You should know that they're here to do your bidding, but they're also expecting to be paid well," Cecil said.

"That's not a problem. Now take me to my men," John said.

Stepping aside, Cecil said, "Take you to them? John, your men are right outside waiting for you."

John exited the office to find seventeen armed men sitting atop horses. "Isn't this a sight for sore eyes!" he yelped.

Samuel, John's former third-in-command, walked forward with his horse. "Major Kemp, your Raiders are all present and accounted for."

"Samuel, my old friend, it's good to see you," John said. "Where have you been all these years?"

"Living in Ole Mexico. I've got some stories to tell you," Samuel said.

"Who's all here?" John asked. "Call out your names," he said, pointing to the man on the far right.

One by one the men shouted their names, with the last man being Franklin Ashe.

"Is that really you, Franklin?" John asked.

"Yes, sir," Franklin said.

"Son, you don't look like the boy I met back in sixty-five," John said.

"No, sir, I'm not that boy," Franklin said, and he was right. He was now a notorious gunman with warrants for his arrest in two states and one territory.

"You all are a sight for sore eyes, let me tell ya." John laughed. "How many came to get rich?"

Every man raised his hand.

"Good, because the reason I've summoned you is to do just that. Sons of the Confederacy, Raiders from

Missouri, we're here to take over this town, make it ours, and get rich as hell!"

The men howled and cheered in unison.

***

His day had started out bad but had ended on a good note with his second well striking oil. He and his men celebrated the gusher as it sprang from the Earth, soaking many of them in thick black oil. To show his appreciation, James invited the men to come with him to the saloon to have a drink.

Upon entering Blackstone's Saloon, they found it packed from wall to wall with a rowdier group than was normal.

James led his men, totaling about fifteen, to the bar and summoned the bartender. "Sal, pour my men each a drink; then keep it coming for as long as they can stand."

Hearing the request, the men cheered.

Sal grabbed several bottles of whiskey, slammed them on the bar, and began filling glasses.

James slapped a fifty-dollar bill on the bar and said, "That should take care of it for the time being. If I owe you more, let me know." He spun around and examined the jovial faces of his crew. He felt such happiness running through his body, heightened because of the recent drama. He was going to enjoy this moment, and nothing was going to stop him.

One by one he handed out the glasses; his men drank and passed them back. Like an assembly line, James would take an empty glass and hand the man a filled one. This went on for ten minutes with short interludes of laughter and chatter with each man who stepped forward.

When he had a small break, he turned, grabbed himself a glass, and tossed it back. He wasn't one for drinking whiskey, but today it didn't matter. He poured himself a fresh glass and went to drink it when a voice from his past hit his ears.

"Well, if it isn't James Harris."

James' hand began to tremble. He set the glass down for fear of spilling it and turned to find Franklin standing behind him. It took him a second to recognize Franklin, but when he did, he asked, "You're here?"

Franklin gave him a scowl and faced off with James.

Fear gripped James. Was this it? Was he about to get gunned down? he asked himself.

With steely eyes focused on James, Franklin placed his hand on the grip of the pistol. "Where's yours?"

"I don't carry a gun," James replied as he contemplated throwing the glass at Franklin.

A smile broke out on Franklin's face. He stepped forward and embraced James tightly. "Hot damn, brother, I didn't think I'd see you here too."

Shocked by the warm greeting, James asked, "What are you doing here?"

"Major Kemp sent for us, said we're going to get rich," Franklin said, pulling back and looking James over from head to toe. "I daresay you look like hell."

James looked down at his clothes; they were filthy with oil and dirt.

"Are you here to get rich with us?" Franklin asked. It was apparent that he hadn't been briefed on the situation in town or John's intentions for James.

"I came here over a year ago," James said.

"Damn, it's good to see you. I know you walked off all huffy that night and, whoa, what a storm of hellfire did that night cause all of us. Did you hear that Major Kemp and Cecil were arrested and sent to prison?"

"I did hear," James said. He was still in shock from the random meeting.

"I know they were angry with you, but I'm sure you've all come to terms, right?"

"We've talked, but I wouldn't say we've come to terms," James said.

"Anyways, I got word two weeks ago that the Raiders were assembling again. I immediately headed west. Word is Major Kemp owns some land and that he's going to drill for oil. I'll admit I don't know a damn thing about it, but if Major Kemp calls, I come," Franklin said. He glanced over James' shoulder and asked, "Care to pass me a glass?"

James reached back, took a glass, and handed it to Franklin.

Not flinching, Franklin tossed it back, wiped his mouth, then howled loudly, "It is good to see you."

James couldn't understand why Franklin was so happy; they had only met for a short time and that was it. He was finding the encounter quite odd.

"So what have you been doing since you left Missouri?" Franklin asked.

"Random jobs here and there," James replied.

"I tried that too, couldn't make any money, so I took up bounty hunting. I do good, but I've had some run-ins with the law on account of my tactics," Franklin said. "I prefer to shoot rather than ask them to surrender."

"Hmm," James said, nodding.

Aaron approached James and said loudly, "Rumor is a group of stinking rebels came to town. That accounts for the saloon being crowded."

James grimaced.

Franklin cocked his head and asked, "Really, there's stinking rebels in here? Where?"

"I think some are over there or maybe them," Aaron answered as he pointed to a group of men huddled in the corner, oblivious to whom he was talking to.

"What should we do about it?" Franklin asked.

"Aaron, how about you make sure the men have their drinks," James said, hoping to stop what he knew was coming.

"Sure thing, boss," Aaron said.

"Say, Aaron," Franklin said, turning Aaron to face him, "did you know James here was a stinking rebel?"

Aaron furrowed his brow and said, "No, he wasn't."

Franklin draped his arm over James' shoulder and said, "Yes, he was. He and I served together."

"Is that true?" Aaron asked.

Feeling his energy ooze out of him, James replied, "That was a long time ago. Now how about going and getting the men drinks."

"You were a Confederate?" Aaron asked.

"He sure was," Franklin said.

"You're not helping," James snarled at Franklin.

Giving him a shocked look, Franklin asked, "Are you not proud of your past or heritage?"

"My past is just that. I'm here in California working oil wells. I don't care about the Confederacy or the Union. I'm here to make money and provide a much-needed resource."

"You're not proud of your father's sacrifice?" Franklin asked.

Aaron stepped back and around James. "I'll get those drinks."

"To be honest, no, what did it get me? Look at what happened to my mother, to me, to our state. We lost the war and my father lost his life. We all ended up worse for it," James said.

"What kind of crap is this I'm hearing? What happened to you?" Franklin asked, taking a step back from James.

"Frank, I left that life a long time ago. I've grown; I've become a husband and a father and a businessman. I don't have a connection to that part of me anymore."

Franklin spat on the floor and said, "To hell with you, James Harris. All that talk from your mouth. I'm sure your pa is rolling in his grave."

"Rolling in his grave. I doubt that. He's buried in some mass grave somewhere in Tennessee," James barked. "The grave marker at our house in Missouri sits over an empty plot. We never got him back; he's gone forever."

"Does Major Kemp know how you feel?" Franklin asked.

"Yeah, he does," James said.

"I thought we were friends, but I can't be friends with someone who hates his past, who looks down upon it," Franklin declared.

Wanting nothing more than to be free of the situation, James said, "It was nice seeing you, Frank."

Franklin spat again. "To hell with you."

James spun around to find Aaron staring.

"You were a Confederate?" Aaron asked.

"Yes, but that is a part of my past. Like I said, I'm not that man anymore; I couldn't care less about any of it. Now if it's going to be a problem for you, then I suggest you go find work somewhere else," James replied bluntly.

Raising his hands, Aaron said, "No, boss, I wasn't expecting to hear that you fought in the war or that you…listen, it doesn't matter; I don't care. You're a good boss, you take care of me and the men, and for that I'm grateful. I was a bit taken aback is all."

"It's fine. Let's get the men some more drinks and enjoy our success today," James said.

Aaron went to work delivering more drinks.

Leaning his weight against the bar, James sighed. Once more he had been confronted with another element from his past. He wasn't sure how this new development would play out, but one thing was sure, it wasn't good.

CHAPTER EIGHT

SEPTEMBER 29, 1876

MENTRYVILLE, CALIFORNIA

For James it was another sleepless night. Plagued by dark thoughts and no answers to the problems he faced, he got up and dressed for the day. It was still dark, but since he couldn't sleep, he thought it best to just go to his old office and gather his things.

He managed to leave the house without waking either Emma or Scarlet, something he was happy about. On his way he took notice of how quiet and peaceful the streets were at this early hour.

Upon arriving, he inserted the key and questioned whether it would work. He turned it, and to his delight the deadbolt clicked and opened up. He stepped across the threshold and into the office. He lit a lantern to find a stack of crates near the door. He peeked inside and noticed the items were his, no doubt packed by William and Christopher. He rummaged through to ensure everything was there, then went to his old desk and searched for anything that might have been left but found nothing.

Satisfied that he had everything, he carried the crates outside only to pause when he looked at his horse. "Darn it, I forgot to bring the wagon," he said out loud. With his thoughts muddled, he had left the house without hitching the wagon. He'd have to leave the crates, go back to his house, and return later. Frustrated, he put the crates back inside, turned and went to leave.

As he turned the key to lock the door, he heard the distinct sound of footfalls coming towards him. He spun around but, due to the dimly lit streets, couldn't see who it was. "Who's there?"

Frantic, William leapt onto the walkway. "Let's get inside, please. I need to talk."

"Talk?" James asked, confused.

"I need to talk to you about something, it's urgent."

"Okay," James said. He unlocked the door and went inside with William just behind him. He walked over to the lantern, but William shouted, "Don't light it."

William then proceeded to draw the blinds.

"I can't see a thing," James complained.

"Ssh," William barked.

When all the blinds were drawn, William said, "Now light the lantern, but keep it low."

James did as he said, then asked, "What's wrong with you? You're acting stranger than normal."

"I, um, I need you to buy my well," William said. Beads of sweat covered his brow.

William's disheveled appearance told James he was in trouble. "Sit down and tell me what is going on," James said.

"Can you or can you not buy my well?" William asked.

"Tell me why you're selling," James said.

Back and forth, William walked the small office space. He ran his fingers through his hair and kept mumbling to himself. "I just need to sell. Can you buy it or not?"

"Why not sell it to Christopher?" James asked, suspecting that he was being conned.

"I asked him; he said no."

"You were just admonishing and taunting me; now you want me to buy your oil operation. No, I won't buy it under these conditions. You have to tell me and then I'll consider it," James said, feeling good that he had some leverage over William.

"On account I need to leave," William said, stopping to give James a hard stare.

"Is something wrong with the well?"

"No, the well is operating fine. I need the money; it's an emergency."

"Why won't Chris buy it?" James again asked.

"You're not listening to me. I need you to buy my well because Chris won't buy it," William yelled.

"Wait, how did you know I was here?"

"I didn't. I was walking back from…it doesn't matter. I saw you coming out of the office, and here we are. Now, will you buy my well or not?"

Taken aback by William's intensity and passion, James leaned back in his chair and replied, "Why are you selling? If you tell me the truth, I'll buy it."

Sitting down, William said, "I'm sorry for how I

treated you. I pray you'll forgive me."

"Not sure if that's enough, but why are you selling and like this? You're drunk, it's evident," James said. He began to think about why William would be in the position and condition he was in now; then it dawned on him what it might be. "It's gambling. You owe someone the money and don't have it."

Tears began to form in William's eyes. "I swear he cheated, but I, um, I couldn't prove it. I don't know how he beat me. I don't understand."

"How much do you owe?" James asked, finding the entire circumstances ironic. Here was the man who not days ago had been accusing him of not having enough money to operate his well, and now he was standing before him, a man who had lost so much he needed to sell the only thing that made him money.

"I owe a lot, okay, but it's not my fault. I swear he cheated, he had to have," William whined as tears flowed down his cheeks.

James took out his handkerchief and tossed it on the desk.

William took it and wiped his face and eyes. "I can only imagine I'm the last person you want to help, but I need the money."

"Who do you owe the money to?" James asked.

"Does it matter? I need to pay him," William said.

"Why did you bet money you didn't have?" James asked.

Springing to his feet, William snapped, "Are you going to help me or not?"

"You're yelling at me about helping when you're in trouble? Where were you? You abandoned me, and now suddenly you need me. What did I say the other day?"

"Just give me five thousand. I'll give you the deed, all the equipment, everything," William said, reaching into his jacket and pulling out a folded piece of paper. He unfolded it and set it on the desk. Pay me five thousand, which I know is half of the value, and I'll sign the deed over to you this very minute."

"I don't know," James said.

"Damn it, James, just give me four, then, please! I said I was sorry. I apologized," William said, his tone changing. "Don't make me beg."

"I just don't know why I should help you. You abandoned me. You went to the very man who threatened me and made a deal with him just to spite me. No, I won't buy your well," James said, getting to his feet.

William lashed out and took James by the arm. "Damn it, James, I need your help."

"I needed your help too, and what did I get from you? Go talk to John Kemp; see if he'll buy it."

"He won't," William said as he let go of James' arm and fell into the chair sobbing.

"And why won't he?"

"I'm in big trouble, Jim. Please help me," William groaned.

"Why won't he buy it?" James asked again.

"'Cause I lost the well in the game. I didn't lose money, I lost the well. I wanted to get what money I could out of it and then leave town," William confessed.

"You were prepared to sell me your well, which you don't even own anymore?" James asked, shocked by the hubris.

"I'm broke, I have nothing, and now the well is gone," William cried.

James looked at William and for a second felt a tinge of sadness for him. Here was a man who let his vice of gambling destroy his life and, to make matters worse, was about to cheat him out of money. "You're despicable. I actually gave honest thought to buying it."

"Lend me some money," William begged.

"No," James replied.

"I know I don't deserve it, but please have pity on me."

In awe at William's audacity, James shook his head and went to the door.

"I'm nothing, a broken man."

"No, you're not, you're just broke. Put your boots back on and go to work, stay out of the saloons and gambling halls, and get it back. You came from nothing, you can do it again," James said, giving him the one gift he could, advice.

"I'm nothing," William sobbed.

"That's not true, Will, you're a turncoat and coward; and you're reaping what you sowed," James said then left the office feeling satisfied that he got the last word over William.

***

"Eyes, everyone, you're looking at the new owner of an oil-producing well just a few miles south of here," Samuel shouted to the other men, who were scattered around the barn that was now their makeshift barracks.

"And where's the deed to this property?" someone asked.

"I'll be getting it shortly, don't you worry," Samuel said, his chest puffed out as he strutted around the barn like a young rooster.

The barn door opened; the light of midday washed over the men inside. In stepped John with Cecil trailing behind him.

"Get to your damn feet!" Cecil hollered.

The men rose.

"Cecil, that's not necessary. We weren't and we're not now regular army. These are my friends now," John said as he sauntered in.

The door closed with a thud.

"I think we need to get you men better accommodations," John said, waving his hand in front of his face. "Is that the smell of animals or you?"

Laughter broke out.

John found a chair, turned it around, and sat down with his arms draped over the back. "I need to discuss with you exactly why you're here and what we're going to be doing."

No one said a word. All eyes were glued on John.

"I summoned you because I need help. I first came

here to exact revenge against a man you'll probably remember…"

"The traitor James Harris!" Franklin shouted from the back of the room.

"Yes, him. After being released from prison, Cecil and I tracked him down to this little town. Our intention at first was to torment him and then, when we'd had our fun, put a bullet in his skull, but then we heard about oil and the riches one could make. Well, I saw an opportunity. I started to ask around and was introduced to a Mexican fella who had land to sell. The irony was he was selling a plot that had real potential, but it was already spoken for by our dear friend James." John cleared his throat and continued, "I left that meeting scheming of a way to get the land and, well, Cecil here came up with the perfect way. Just before the deal was finalized, we told Garcia about James' notorious past with hopes that it would play to his moral side. To our benefit it did, and we swooped in and bought it. Now we're the owners of a large piece of land with rugged slopes and mountains."

"Are you wanting us to work for you to find oil on it?" someone asked.

"Yes, you'll work for me in that capacity, but first I need something else from you. Our issue is I don't know a damn thing about finding much less drilling for oil, but there are crews that do. What I need is for you to go out in town and do what's necessary to get those crews to work for us. I don't care if you have to harass, intimidate, lie, cheat, whatever; just get those men to come work for us. I also want to acquire the other oil rights around here. I own that one piece of land and now most of the lots and buildings in town, but I want it all."

"What do we get out of it?" someone asked.

"I will share everything we make with you. I've had Cecil here draft an agreement that stipulates this arrangement. Each one of you will get a percentage of all the operations we set up or acquire, with me and Cecil owning the majority."

Several men began to crosstalk.

"Quiet!" Cecil barked.

The room grew instantly silent.

John smiled and went on, "I think the future for this state and others is oil, and I won't settle for a small part, I want it all. Does everyone understand what I'm asking of them?"

Nods and shouts of yes came from the group.

"Good, go out and do what's necessary. I need to get crews heading out to that new plot as soon as possible, and like I said, do what is necessary."

No one said a word.

"Well, you heard him, get off your asses and go out there. Find the crews; best to go out to where they work and recruit them right there," Cecil hollered. "Go, get up, get off your asses, and get to work."

The men all jumped to their feet and headed to the door.

As Samuel walked by, John called out, "I hear you own a well now."

Stopping, Samuel replied, "Yes, sir."

"How did you come to acquire this?" John asked.

"Poker game," Samuel answered happily.

"Won it by chance," John said.

"No, by skill," Samuel countered.

Crossing his arms, John asked, "How is that?"

"Poker is a game of skill. I know how to read cards and players. I've been playing a lot since the end of the war and have gotten very good."

"Where is this well?" John asked.

"I don't know. I haven't seen the deed for the property yet; the man is supposed to bring it to me later today," Samuel said.

John shot a glance to Cecil, who started laughing loudly.

Samuel too started to laugh.

"You have no idea what we think is humorous, do you?" John asked.

An awkward look spread across Samuel's face. "Because I won the well?"

"No, it's because you had a man use a piece of property as a bet without seeing the deed. How do you know he wasn't lying?" John asked.

Samuel immediately stopped talking. "Oh."

John patted him on the back and said, "I thought you said you were experienced."

"I am," Samuel said.

"Doesn't sound like it." Cecil chuckled.

"It'll be fine. You learned something today," John said.

The three exited the barn and spilled out onto the street.

A large crowd had gathered farther down the street.

John stopped a passerby and asked, "What's the commotion?"

"A man hanged himself," the man answered.

Curious, the three walked up.

When Samuel saw who was hanging from the post, his mouth opened wide.

"What's that pinned to his chest?" Cecil asked, referring to a piece of paper that was dangling from the man's shirt.

Samuel broke through the crowd, snatched the paper from his chest, and walked back, reading it as he came.

"What is it?" John asked.

Holding it up, Samuel said, "The deed to my oil well."

John exploded in laughter. "That's the man you beat last night in poker?"

"The very one," Samuel said happily as he folded the paper up and shoved it into his pocket.

With a wide grin stretched across his face, John said, "You, my friend, are one lucky son of a bitch."

***

Getting up from the dinner table, James rushed to the door to see who was knocking. He peeked out the side window and saw it was Christopher. He opened the door and said, "What can I do for you?"

"William is dead," Christopher answered, his eyes moist with tears.

Turning ashen, James said, "Come in."

Christopher removed his hat and stepped over the threshold.

"Are you hungry?" James asked.

"No."

"Go take a seat in the parlor. I need to tell Emma to continue eating without me," James said and rushed off. He returned promptly and joined Christopher. "What happened?"

"He took his own life," Christopher said.

"How?"

"It was the middle of the day. He rode his horse up to a post, tied a rope to it, and let the horse run. There were countless eyewitnesses."

"He did it in broad daylight?" James asked, shocked by the news.

"I didn't know he was that distraught. I spoke to him very early this morning; he came to my house. I could tell he'd been drinking. He asked if I wanted to buy his well, but I declined. He knows, you know, I don't operate like that."

"I saw him too, but later than you did. I also declined to purchase. When he came to me, he was frantic."

Putting his face in his hands, Christopher said, "Had I known he was going to kill himself, I would have helped him, maybe loaned him the money."

"He didn't need the money. He had lost the deed to his well in a poker game. He came to see us to sell it. Yes, you heard that right; he came to swindle us."

"No."

"Yes, he finally admitted what he was doing.

Apparently, he was broke, and the last thing he had of value was the well, but he lost that too. He was hoping to sell it to one of us; then he planned on leaving town," James said.

"I can't believe he'd do that to me...us," Christopher said, sickened by the bombshell news.

"The entire thing, this past week, has shaken all of us, but it appears William was a man we really couldn't trust."

"I apologize for my treatment of you, James, and I wish to reconcile right this second."

"You do? What will Belinda say?" James asked.

"It doesn't matter. You're right, this week has been disturbing, but I can't do it without friends. Will you forgive me for my actions?"

James thought about the apology.

"I'll understand if you don't accept it, but know that I'm truly sorry and want us to work together again," Christopher said.

Knowing he could use some allies, James stuck out his hand and said, "I forgive you, friend."

Christopher took James' hand and said, "Friends....again."

"Now can I offer you some roast?"

"I can't. I need to get home," Christopher said, getting to his feet. He went to the door, but just before leaving, he said, "William didn't have any next of kin, so I'll take his remains and hold a funeral for him. Knowing that he tried to defraud me is unsettling, but no man should be without a proper funeral."

"You're a good person, Chris," James said. He did like

Christopher and believed he was a good person; hence why he was perplexed by his initial treatment of him.

"It's the right thing to do," Christopher said. "I'll have him buried the day after tomorrow and have services at St. John's Church. It would be nice if you and Emma could attend."

"We'll be there."

Putting his hat back on, Christopher exited the house. He turned and said, "Tell Emma I said hello."

"I will."

Christopher disappeared into the darkness.

After he closed the door, James stood frozen to the spot. Each day kept bringing more disturbing news or unforeseen revelations. Deep down he could feel the tempo was increasing and suspected it would all come to an epic conclusion. He just hoped he was still standing when it was all over.

CHAPTER NINE

SEPTEMBER 30, 1876

MENTRYVILLE, CALIFORNIA

With the wagon hitched, James went to grab lumber to finish the oil well tower at site number two and build a cabin for the men who would stay there and work.

"Thank you for the order, Mr. Harris," Michael Smith, the owner of the lumberyard, said. "Pull the wagon around back, and we'll get you loaded up."

"Okay," James said. He headed out the door and walked right into a man on the walkway. "Excuse me."

The man shoved him. "If it isn't the traitor of Independence."

James' eyes widened upon hearing the name of the town where the incident had occurred years before. Around him he saw six men. He didn't recognize five of them, but the sixth he did; it was Franklin.

"Hi, Jimbo," Franklin said before taking a bite out of

an apple.

"What do you want?" James asked.

"We saw you from across the street and thought we'd come say hello," Franklin said. "Do you remember Billy, Timothy, Roger, Art, and Cass. They're all Raiders like you were."

"What do you want?" James asked again.

"Say, I heard about your partner, so sad," Franklin said as he pretended to wipe a tear. "So, so sad."

James ignored Franklin. He pushed past Timothy and Art and went to the wagon but was stopped by Billy, who stood directly in front of him.

"Hi," Billy said, a toothless grin on his face.

"Move," James growled.

Franklin jumped off the walkway and stepped over next to James. "Did you buy yourself some wood in there?"

"Leave me be," James barked.

"You know something, Jimbo, I can't do that," Franklin said. "Is it okay if I call you that? James is so formal, and being that we're friends, I think Jim or Jimbo works."

"Just leave me be and I'll leave you be," James said.

A stack of three-foot-long stakes were piled near the front door. Franklin nodded to Timothy to grab one.

Timothy picked up a stake and tossed it to Franklin. "Here ya go, Frank."

Franklin grabbed the stake and held it firmly in his grasp. "Why, thank you, Tim."

Timothy tossed the other men stakes.

Fear ran through James, he'd escaped a physical

altercation so far, but now it appeared his luck had run out. He tried to push past Billy but was shoved back.

"You and I need to discuss your behavior the other night. In fact, we need to talk about that night eleven years ago," Franklin said.

Knowing he needed to get out of there, James spun and tried to walk past Franklin but again was prevented.

"You're not going anywhere, Jimbo," Franklin teased.

"Just let me go, okay, Frank," James said, his hands raised high, showing he didn't want to fight.

Franklin looked down at the stake in his hand and said, "Is this pine?" He put it to his nose and sniffed. "Yep, smells like pine."

"I don't want trouble," James said.

The other men surrounded him.

"Frank, this isn't a good idea; townsfolk won't take kindly to you hurting a productive member of this town," James said, trying anything to get away from what he knew was coming.

"Thing is, I am looking for trouble and so are these other men. We're upset, angry really, at how you left us all those years ago. And now I come to find out that Major Kemp and Cecil were locked away because of what you did."

"You were there. I had to do it," James said.

"I was there. I just didn't know you were the reason they were put in prison. Knowing that and your behavior the other night has me reconsidering our past friendship," Franklin said.

James made a quick dash but like the last two times

didn't get anywhere.

Franklin shoved James hard against his wagon, then swung the stake, striking James in the stomach. "How did that feel?"

James bent over in pain from the strike.

Franklin stepped back and said, "Let him have it."

The other five man lifted their stakes and began to pummel James, who dropped to his knees.

The men kept up their assault, battering him ruthlessly.

James turned and tried to crawl under the wagon, but Franklin grabbed his ankle and pulled him back out, where he was struck again numerous times. Crying out, James shouted, "Help!"

Franklin began to laugh loudly as he watched James lie on the ground, his arms covering the back of his head.

A towering shadow cast over James, catching Franklin's attention. He looked to his right and saw an ominous-looking man. It was Rig.

Rig reached out and grasped Billy's arm in mid-swing. He squeezed hard, pulled him close, and slammed his forehead into Billy's face. The impact shattered Billy's nose and sent him sprawling backwards.

Seeing what Rig had done, Franklin howled, "Who the hell are you?"

Rig faced Franklin, cracked a smile, reeled back his right arm, and punched him.

Franklin reeled from the punch, tripped on the walkway, and fell down.

The other men came at Rig, with Art charging him

first. Timing it just right, Rig stepped to the side, took Art's arm, cranked it back, and pried the stake from his grasp. Now armed with a stake himself, he spun it around and smashed it into the back of Art's head. The blow from Rig sent him crashing into the hard ground.

Timothy jumped at Rig, the stake held high above his head. He came down, but Rig blocked the blow, kicked Timothy in the groin, then followed up by hitting him in the jaw with the stake. Timothy fell to his knees and spat out several teeth. Not done with him, Rig swung up. This time the stake struck Timothy just below the nose. The strike was brutal, severing the lower part of Timothy's nose. He fell over onto his back and cried out in pain.

Cass came at Rig; he swung and made contact, hitting Rig in the shoulder.

Rig gave him a deadly stare, swung his stake, and hit Cass in the side of the neck. Then swung again, this time coming from overhead, and came down on top of Cass' head.

Cass' eyes rolled back into his head. He dropped to the ground unconscious.

Rig spun around and surveyed the carnage to find he'd taken out all but Roger, who stood back stunned and wide-eyed. "You're next," Rig said.

"I don't have any beef with you," Roger said. He tossed his stake on the ground.

From underneath the wagon, James gawked at the scene that had just unfolded. He didn't know who the man was who had just saved him, but would make sure he found out. "Thank you."

"Stay put. These gentlemen may not be done just yet," Rig said, motioning for James to remain under the wagon.

Franklin got to his feet and wiped the small amount of blood from his split lip. "I should kill you right here and right now."

"I wouldn't do that if I were you, you'll only end up getting yourself killed," Rig warned.

Billy scurried from the ground and launched himself towards Rig.

With a smooth fluidity, Rig spun around and swung the stake like a bat. He connected with Billy's jaw and sent him back to the ground, his face hitting first.

"Who's next?" Rig asked, spinning back to face Franklin. "You?"

"Whoever you are, just know that we're not through with you," Franklin spat.

"You should pick up your men and head back to wherever you came from," Rig said. "You should also think about turning your life around. If you keep down this path, you'll end up six feet under."

"Help get Cass, and you, Roger, pick Billy up," Franklin ordered.

Slowly, Franklin and his men got up and departed the scene, leaving Rig and James to talk.

"It's safe now," Rig said, offering a hand to help James up.

Taking it, James got to his feet and dusted himself off. He ached and throbbed; he couldn't count how many times he'd been hit, but knew his body would be covered in bruises. A sudden sense of gratitude swept over him. If it hadn't been for Rig, he could have ended up severely wounded or, worse, dead. "I need to thank you."

"It's what I do," Rig said, tossing the stake he still held onto the ground.

"You rescue people? That's what you do?" James snorted.

"Yes, that's exactly what I do," Rig said.

"Then I'm grateful for your occupation and that you happened along," James said. He found it hard not to stare at Rig's face.

"Will you be okay now?"

"I think so. I was getting some lumber, but I think I'll head home and get cleaned up."

"Is there a hotel you recommend?" Rig asked.

"Oh, you need a place to stay?"

"I do, just for a short period of time."

"You should stay with me and my family. We have a spare room, and my wife cooks amazingly well. It's the least I can do," James offered.

"I wouldn't want to impose."

"I won't take no for an answer," James insisted.

Rig thought about the offer for a moment. He normally would say no, but his gut told him to go, and when his instinct told him something, it was best to listen. "My horse is over there. I'll follow you."

Grinning, James slowly climbed onto the wagon. "Wait."

On his way to get Fire, Rig stopped and turned. "Yes?"

"What's your name?"

"Rig, you can call me Rig."

***

"What do you mean one man did this?" Cecil howled.

"I'd like to say it was more, but it wasn't," Franklin answered.

"We need to find him and teach him a lesson."

"I should have shot him down."

"Maybe you should have, but it's too late for that," Cecil said.

In the corner of the room, John sat staring at a map of the land he'd just acquired. He was listening but wasn't overly concerned.

"John, are you hearing this?" Cecil asked.

John lifted his head and replied, "I am."

"I'm going to head out, find this fella, and put a round in him," Cecil snapped.

"Don't do that," John said calmly.

Eyes wide, Cecil asked, "Why not? He just beat six of our men. Cass still hasn't woken up."

"I want you to go out and find him. He seems like a formidable man; maybe we can bring him over to our side."

"But he did this protecting James," Cecil challenged.

"Maybe he did, but it doesn't mean he knows the man. He could merely be a Good Samaritan."

"A what?" Cecil asked.

"What's a Samaritan?" Franklin queried.

"Haven't you all read the Bible before?" John asked,

confused they hadn't heard the term before.

"I'm surprised you have," Cecil quipped.

"Never mind what a Samaritan is. I want to meet this man; he seems intriguing," John said, putting his attention back on the map.

"Whatever you say," Cecil said.

"And didn't I hear you mention something about his face?" John asked as he used his finger to trace a contour line on the map.

"Half his face looks like it's been melted off. If I met him in a dark alley, I could easily mistake him for some sort of monster," Franklin said.

"Go find him; bring him to me. I'd like to meet this monster who slayed six of my men," John said.

Cecil kicked the chair Franklin was seated in and said, "Well, you heard him. Go find your monster and bring him here."

Franklin got up and left the hotel room.

"What do you think?" John asked, referencing the story.

"I think he's telling the truth. Why would he admit to being beaten by a single man?" Cecil asked.

"True. Say, when is that funeral for that fella happening?"

"Tomorrow morning, I read."

"Good, we're going," John said.

"Why on earth would we go to that man's funeral?"

Facing Cecil, John replied, "On account that I need to make an announcement to those distinguished members of the town, and I can't think of a better opportunity than when they're all assembled in one place."

***

Emma pulled James into the kitchen and whispered, "You invited that man to stay in our house without consulting me?"

"I didn't think I'd have to do that considering he saved my life. I thought you'd want to thank him and show some gratitude," James snapped.

With her jaw clenched tightly, Emma paced the kitchen.

"Is it that big a problem?" James asked.

She stopped and answered, "Yes. I understand you're the man of the house, but that sort of decision requires my input."

"He saved my life, Emma," James countered.

In the dining room, Rig sat at the table opposite Scarlet, who couldn't stop smiling at Rig.

"I think they're talking about me," Rig quipped.

"My ma does sound mad." Scarlet giggled.

"I can barely hear them, but I don't think she's happy either," Rig joked.

Back in the kitchen, Emma kept pacing. "With everything that happened, you think it's wise to invite a complete stranger into our home and have him stay here?"

"I do. Out of all the horrible things that have happened, he's the one thing that is really good. I could have been killed today. That man risked his life; he handily commenced beating six of John's men. It was quite a sight," James exclaimed, his voice rising.

"Be quiet," Emma barked, her voice now matching his.

"Rig is staying and that's that," James said. "Now let's go back and sit down. We're being rude to our guest."

Grabbing his arm, Emma asked, "Look at his face. What happened to him?"

"I don't know, but don't stare."

"He scares me."

Taking her into his arms, he said, "If I thought this man meant you or Scarlet harm, I wouldn't have invited him. I don't know how to explain it, but I feel safe around him."

Giggling came from the dining room.

James smiled and continued, "And I think Scarlet likes him too."

"Can you promise next time you'll consult me?" Emma asked.

"I can't make that promise on account this happened like it did. Sometimes things aren't convenient or don't go as we'd like. I need you to be more flexible."

"James Harris, if I'm one thing, it's flexible. You forget your manners and use your tongue harshly."

"I stand corrected and I apologize," James said. "Now please, let's go back to dinner."

She nodded.

The two returned to find Rig making shadow puppets on the wall and Scarlet laughing hysterically.

"You look like you're having fun," James said, taking a seat at the head of the table.

Emma feigned a smile and took her seat at the opposite end from James. She extended her arm for the potatoes, but they were just out of reach. Rig picked up the bowl and handed them to her. "Here you go, ma'am."

"Thank you," she said sweetly.

Rig shyly looked around the table and knew he needed to address the awkwardness in the room. "Before we dig into this fine meal, let me say that I'm thankful for the meal and for your hospitality. I'm especially thankful to you, Mrs. Harris. I know having a stranger in your home can be unsettling, especially a stranger who looks like this…"

"Oh, please, don't say—"

He waved her off and continued, "I'm aware that my appearance is off-putting, and I'm comfortable with how people look at me. I've lived like this for a long time, but it needs to be said that if my presence here will cause undue stress and worry, I do not mind going into town to find adequate accommodations. When Mr. Harris—"

"Call me James."

"When James invited me, I first declined, but I had a sense, no, more like a premonition, that I should come because what happened today will happen again and that you'll need me."

"You think they'll try to hurt James again?" Emma asked.

"I do," Rig confirmed.

The room went silent.

"I look at it this way. We were meant to meet because I was sent here."

"What do you mean you were sent here?" James

asked, curious about Rig's statement.

"I don't want to get into the how, but know that I'm here now and I'll do whatever is in my power to ensure your family is safe," Rig said.

"Mr..."

"Just call me Rig, nothing more."

"Rig, I'm sure you overheard me in the kitchen. Please forgive me," Emma said.

"There's nothing to forgive, Mrs. Harris. I'm a big and ugly fella, and I scare most people."

"I don't think you're scary," Scarlet blurted out.

Rig gave her a smile.

"You're welcome to stay as long as you'd like," Emma said, smiling, the conversation easing her concerns.

"I for one am glad we met when we did," James said.

"Now that that's out of the way, shall we dine on this fabulous-looking meal?" Rig asked.

"Yes, please, dig in," James said.

Scarlet jumped up from the table and rushed to James' side. She leaned over and whispered in his ear, "I told you our guardian angel was coming."

CHAPTER TEN

OCTOBER 1, 1876

MENTRYVILLE, CALIFORNIA

The priest closed the Bible, looked at the people assembled in the pews, and said, "This concludes the requiem mass. We will now take the casket to the graveyard for burial. Thank you for coming."

Christopher sat for a moment and thought, was that it? That was all he was going to say about someone's life? He found it hard to fathom that someone could live thirty years only to have a twenty-minute mass serve as a memorial, and out of that twenty only a brief eulogy that lasted no more than three minutes summed up William's life.

He had only known William for a little over a year, but in that time he'd grown to like him a lot. Of course, he had his problems, and many saw William's bad side, his anger especially, but Christopher found him charming many times. If William was anything, he was witty and charming, with many describing him as fun to be around. This was the side he saw mostly and came to like.

James cleared his throat to get Christopher's attention.

Snapping out of his daydream, Christopher stood and walked to the front of the church, followed by James, Aaron and a friend of Christopher's who'd volunteered to help carry the casket.

Just before reaching the front of the church, the doors opened in the back.

The light of midday swept across the spacious church and filled every dark corner.

Everyone, seated or not, turned to see who was coming in.

Strutting in with confidence was John Kemp. He walked up to the holy water but instead of dipping a finger, he soaked both of his hands and wiped them on a handkerchief.

Gasps and light chatter broke out.

"I say, who are you, sir?" said the priest, a man by the name of Father Hill.

Flooding in just behind John were fourteen of his men. They split off, with half going to the left and the other half heading up the right side. Like sentries standing a post, they had their backs to the wall and faced everyone sitting in the pews.

The chatter increased in volume.

"I say, what is the meaning of this?" Father Hill blared, his tone turning angry.

"I'll just be a moment, Father," John said.

"This is a sacred funeral," Hill barked. He stepped from the altar and headed towards John. Just before he got to within arm's length, Cecil stepped out in front of John with his pistol in his hand. He cocked it and aimed it in between Father Hill's eyes. "Just hold up right there."

Father Hill froze. He stuttered a few words that were unintelligible and held his hands up.

The people gathered in the pews began to stir, with many of the women displaying fear.

John walked around Cecil, put his hand on Father Hill's shoulder, and shouted, "I waited until the service was over, so I did show respect for that poor fellow up there."

James stared in horror. He thought of rushing down and stopping John, but seeing all the men, several of them being the ones who beat him, made him decide to stay put.

"Now that I've got everyone's attention," John shouted.

Looking to Emma, who was seated near the front, her eyes pleading with him to do something, James acted. "You're not wanted here!"

Feigning as if he couldn't make out who said it, John squinted, bobbed his head around slightly, and said, "Is that you, James?"

"You and your men need to leave," James said. He advanced towards John, who was now standing a quarter of the way down the center aisle.

Franklin, who was standing along the wall, tore through a row of pews, stopping in front of James. "You're not going any farther."

Unable to proceed unless he was going to fight Franklin, James stopped.

"James, I'm here to make an announcement to the finest folk of this town, and I imagined the most efficient way of doing so was to wait until they were all gathered together at once," John explained.

The chatter from those seated grew in volume.

John took a few more steps, a large smile creasing his slender face. "I promise you, I'm not here to be disrespectful. I'm here now because it's the one time I could get you all gathered in one place. Many of you are business owners; you run shops, are tradesmen, and some of you, like Mr. Harris up there, run an oil-drilling operation. If you didn't know, I'm now in the oil business, having purchased the Santa Teresa parcel from Mr. Garcia. Some of you have no doubt heard about that. I'm here today though for an entirely different matter. I'm here to offer those other oilmen a buyout. Yes, you heard that right, I want to buy your well."

"John, you need to go," James called out.

Returning James' plea to leave with a broad smile, John continued, "Who here wants to sell to me?"

No one raised their hand.

"I can't believe no one wants to sell. How about you tell me what you want, and we can make a deal?" John said.

"I don't know what you're doing, but this is inappropriate. If you thought you could come here and get people to sell you their wells, you're mistaken. These are good people. They came to pay their respects, not wheel and deal."

"Seven thousand," a man called out from the center of the church.

Loud gasps rang out.

"You clearly don't know your neighbors," John said with a sneer on his face directed at James. Turning towards the man, he said, "Meet me later and we can discuss it. My office is located just down off Main Street. I'm in the same building Mr. Garcia used."

"Very well," the man said.

"Does anyone else wish to sell their wells?" John asked.

Fed up with John's antics, Christopher mustered the courage and marched from the casket down the center aisle towards John, only to be stopped when Franklin tore his pistol from his holster and pointed it at him. "Stay right there."

Unafraid, Christopher shouted, "Get out of here!"

"There's no need to yell. We're in a house of God," John quipped.

"Leave," Christopher said.

James thought about how he could tackle this problem but couldn't come up with a response that wouldn't end up getting him shot. With many of John's men in the church and heavily armed, any attempt to remove John would be met with deadly force.

Ignoring Christopher, John again called out, "Does anyone else want to sell their wells? I think it should be known that I'll pay fair market value and that this offer expires at the end of the day."

"Are you done?" James asked.

Surveying the crowd, John replied, "I am...for now."

"Leave," James said.

"Say, where's your friend?"

"Who?" James asked, fully knowing who John was asking about.

"The man who jumped in and saved you from the rightful beating you deserved," John said.

At first James was reluctant to say but found having a man as fearsome as Rig on his side was too tempting not to show off. "He's down the street getting something to eat at Ruthie's." The second he uttered it, he regretted saying anything.

"Eating was more important than showing respect to the great William Edington?"

"He didn't know the man," James said.

John walked up to within a few feet of James and examined his cuts, bruises and scrapes. "They didn't hurt you too bad."

"That'll be different next time, I swear," Franklin said, his comment directed at James.

"Go!" James barked, his anger beginning to show.

John spit tobacco juice on the wood floor, gave James one last devilish grin, turned and exited the church. On his way out he stopped, patted Father Hill on the back, and said, "Nice church you have here." He disappeared into the bright light, with his men filing out right behind him, except for Franklin.

"I'm not done with you," Franklin sneered and raced towards the entrance.

"What are we going to do about him?" Christopher

asked, referring to John.

"I don't know yet," James answered.

Emma tugged on James' arm. "You need to go warn Rig."

"You're right," James said and headed for the door.

"Where are you going? What about William?" Christopher cried out.

"I need to warn Rig," James said, sprinting out of the church. He hit the street and saw it was too late. Up ahead were Franklin, Timothy, Cass, and Art walking into Ruthie's restaurant. "Damn!" he yelped.

***

Rig enjoyed the pie, savoring the last bite. It had been a long time since he'd eaten a slice of apple pie, but each time he did, it brought him back to his childhood.

"Will that be all?" Ruthie asked, her hands on her hips, staring down at Rig.

"Yes, ma'am, that'll do," Rig answered.

Ruthie was a large woman; no doubt she enjoyed much of her own cooking. She picked up his plate and said, "That'll be five cents."

"That's a great price," Rig said, digging into his vest pocket. He pulled out a dollar and handed it to her. "Keep the change."

Her eyes widened. "Are you sure, dear?"

"I'm positive. Your food was delicious and your company superb. It's not every day that I'm received with such warmth," Rig said. The second he walked into the restaurant, he wasn't treated any differently than any other customer and didn't receive an awkward stare or glance, something he wasn't accustomed to.

"You are a doll, thank you. Now you make sure you come back in here for my biscuits and gravy. I use the best sausage and a touch of bacon for my gravy; gives it a proper taste," she said.

"I'll be sure to stop by."

Ruthie sauntered off slowly, her large frame squeezing in between tables.

Rig leaned back and admired the quaint place. No more than six tables were able to fit in the dining room, with a short bar at the far end, opposite the front door. Behind the bar, like in many other drinking establishments, hung a mirror. Rig glanced in it to see Franklin and some other men he'd beaten just yesterday coming towards the entrance of the restaurant.

He leaned towards a couple seated next to him and said, "I suggest you take cover behind the bar or in the back."

The couple gave him an odd look.

Rig pulled his pistol and set it on the table.

Seeing the firearm, the couple sprang to their feet and raced to the kitchen.

Ruthie appeared, saw Rig was armed, and asked, "What on earth are you doing?"

"Ruthie, see those men coming? They're headed here to kill me, I suspect. I recommend you go take shelter in the back."

She looked through the large paned-glass window and

saw Franklin and his men closing in. She could tell by their appearances they were mean and ornery men, no doubt hell-bent on causing trouble. "What about you?"

Rig smiled and said, "It's not my time to die. I'll be fine."

Finding his response eerie in its tone, she rushed back through the door and into the kitchen, leaving Rig sitting alone, his back to the front door.

Franklin, with the others just behind him, reached the front door. He peered inside and saw Rig sitting at a table next to the bar. "He's just sitting there. His damn back is facing us. We've got him."

"Stop!" James hollered.

Hearing James, Franklin turned to Al and ordered, "Shut him up." Turning to the other two, he said, "Follow me inside."

Cass and Timothy nodded. Both were nervous about the pending altercation with the man who had bested them all just the day before.

Al drew his pistol, cocked it, and took aim on James.

Seeing Al draw down on him, James stopped his advance and put up his hands. "Don't shoot."

"He's not coming this way anymore," Al said.

"Let's go, boys," Franklin said. With his pistol Lucille in his hands, he opened the door and rushed inside but found the place empty and Rig gone. "Wait, he was just here."

Cass and Timothy came in just behind him; both parroted Franklin, "Where did he go?" Timothy's voice was muddled, as his nose was heavily bandaged and he was missing several teeth from the encounter yesterday.

"He must have slipped out the back," Franklin said, pointing to the kitchen door. "Go get him."

Cass and Timothy shoved chairs and tables out of their way, their singular focus the door to the kitchen. What they didn't know was Rig had taken the opportunity of Franklin's delay at the front door to address James to slip behind the bar. There he found a double barrel shotgun sitting on a shelf. He confirmed it was loaded and planned on using it.

"We'll find the bastard," Cass barked, picking up a chair in his way and throwing it across the restaurant.

Rig jumped to his feet and asked, "You looking for me?"

Cass' and Timothy's heads pivoted towards Rig, a look of shock on their faces.

Rig cocked both hammers back, quickly aimed at Cass, and pulled the forward trigger. The shotgun roared. Buckshot exploded out the muzzle and struck Cass in the chest. The force from the blast sent him backwards and through a window.

Timothy nervously cocked his pistol, almost dropping it, and went to raise it, but not before Rig pulled the second trigger on the shotgun. Like the first blast, this shot collided into Timothy's chest. He reeled back off his feet and onto a table. He gasped once then died.

Franklin raised his pistol and hastily fired his first shot, missing Rig by inches.

Undeterred, Rig stood his ground, not flinching.

Franklin cocked Lucille, his Remington model 1859,

aimed and shot; again he missed. "Damn. What's going on?" he asked loudly, glancing at his pistol. He had always been a good shot, rarely missing.

Taking advantage of Franklin's apparent disarray, Rig threw the empty shotgun at him. The shotgun hit Franklin in the shoulder and almost made him drop Lucille. With Franklin fumbling his pistol, Rig drew his Colt, cocked it and aimed.

Seeing Rig aiming, Franklin took control of Lucille with both hands and cocked it, praying that Rig wouldn't shoot him before he could get one more off.

Rig fired.

Franklin jumped, looked down at his chest, expecting to see a hole, but found none.

A thump sounded from outside; it was Art. Rig had fired and hit him.

Thinking he still had a chance, Franklin got Lucille cocked and raised the pistol, to see Rig once more aiming, this time at him. He and Rig fired at the same time.

Franklin felt searing pain in his chest and the warmth of the blood coming from the wound. He'd been hit and badly. He dropped to his knees and coughed up a large amount of blood.

Rig marched from behind the bar and up to Franklin. "Do you repent for your sins?"

"How is it you're not hurt?" Franklin asked, coughing up more blood.

"It's not my time," Rig answered. "Now, do you repent for your sins?"

"Sin? Go to hell," Franklin said as his right thumb

fumbled to cock Lucille back once more.

"Don't try it," Rig said.

Getting Lucille cocked, Franklin muttered, "Die, you son of a—"

Rig put his pistol to Franklin's head and pulled the trigger just as James burst through the door.

The back of Franklin's head exploded and his body went limp.

Shocked by the scene, James stood frozen to the spot.

Rig holstered his pistol and said, "James, are you okay?"

"I'm fine, you?" James asked.

"Fine," Rig answered. He looked around the restaurant and frowned at the damage done to Ruthie's restaurant.

The kitchen door opened and out stepped Ruthie, a cleaver in her grasp. Seeing Rig in the dining area over a dead body and another bloody body on a table, she gasped loudly. "My restaurant."

Rig turned and said, "I'll help you get this cleaned up."

"But the window, the furniture, how will I pay for it all?" she asked, tears coming to her eyes.

Rig walked over, pulled his wallet from his jacket pocket, opened it, and removed a stack of cash. "Will two hundred pay for the damage?"

"Why are you giving me money?" she asked.

James too found the offer surprising.

"I feel bad, and I have too much of this as it is,"

Rig said, handing the cash to her. "Take it, please."

She took the money and asked, "Who are you?"

"I'm just a man who likes your cookin'. Now please use that money to get the place cleaned up. I want to come back in the morning and get those biscuits and gravy."

***

The barn that John's men used as a barracks was unusually still. The men watched in silence as John paced back and forth in front of the bodies of Franklin, Art, Cass and Timothy.

Cecil himself was quiet, which told everyone that John was on the verge of a rare but violent outburst.

John stopped his pacing and looked to the men huddled. "Did I not say I wanted to meet this mysterious man?" he asked, referring to Rig.

The men remained silent.

"Well?"

Nods and verbal acknowledgments came from the group.

"Then why do I have four of my men dead? Huh? Why were four of my men killed trying to murder the very man I said I wished to meet with?" John asked, his voice strained.

"They wanted revenge," Cecil blurted out.

John spun around and shouted, "I know what their small minds wanted, but did they once think about what I wanted?"

"No, sir," Cecil replied.

"I wanted to meet this man on my terms. He seemed from the first encounter like a man to be reckoned with, someone whom I could turn, but now that may not be possible. He will no doubt think I sent these fools to kill him. If one man can best six of mine in a fistfight, and then again single-handedly best four of them in an outmatched gunfight, I want him on our side," John said. "Where are the other two?"

Roger and Billy raised their hands.

"Don't you dare think about doing something so foolish. You do as I say. If I want him killed, then I'll order it," John barked.

Both men nodded.

"Cecil, what have you found out about him?" John asked.

"Not much. We know he's badly scarred; it appears half of his body had been badly burned. As far as where he comes from, I don't know," Cecil answered.

"Since I clearly need to act quickly, I want you to go summon him. I wish to speak with this gentleman immediately. Find him and make it happen," John said.

"Yes, sir," Cecil said, not moving.

"I said immediately, so go…now!" John howled.

Cecil sprang to his feet and rushed out of the barn.

John gazed upon the dead men, stopping at Franklin. "You had promise, but you allowed your damn hubris to get in the way."

"Where should I bury them?" Samuel asked.

"Bury? Throw them in a ditch," John said.

"We're not going to give them a proper burial?"

Samuel asked.

"These men violated my trust and yours. No, take them somewhere and toss their bodies in a ditch like I said. Let this be a lesson for the rest of you. We've come to this town to change our lives, and we're on the cusp of doing so, but you have to do as I say. This isn't Missouri; we can't conduct ourselves like we did during the war and after. This doesn't mean we won't be forceful when we need to be, but if we're to become wealthy, we'll need to become a bit more legitimate. Does everyone understand?"

The men nodded.

"Now go do whatever Cecil has you doing, and again, I best not hear about you doing one thing, no matter how small, that strays from what we're trying to do here," John barked.

Samuel had several men help him haul off the bodies while the remaining men departed the barn.

John followed the men out and onto the street. He watched the townspeople come and go. In a matter of days he'd become a major player in the town, and he would not allow the actions of his men to steer him off course. He was an outlaw and a killer, but he knew if he was to truly take advantage of what he'd already gotten, he would have to change. This didn't mean that he also couldn't seek the retribution he so wanted from James. Like planned, he would kill him slowly by bleeding him out financially.

***

Rig shuffled the deck of cards and fanned them out. "Pick

a card."

Scarlet sat and thought. "Any card?"

"Any card you'd like," Rig replied.

James and Emma sat in the love seat across from them, both happy to be home and safe after the events of the day.

"This one," Scarlet said, pointing at a card near the center.

"Pull it out," Rig said.

Scarlet did as he said and looked at it.

"Don't show the card to me, but show it to your parents," Rig said.

She did as he said.

"Put the card back in the deck, anywhere you want," Rig said.

With a giggle, she slid it near the front.

Rig took the deck, shuffled the cards, and set them on the table. "Cut the deck."

"Cut?"

"That means to separate a part of the deck, like this," Rig said, taking half of the deck and setting it to the side.

"Oh, I see," Scarlet replied. She was mesmerized by everything that was happening.

"Now put the other half on top," Rig ordered.

Scarlet did exactly as he said. Looking towards her parents, she squealed with excitement. "This is so much fun."

Rig picked up the deck and began to place the cards facedown. He stopped at one, paused, and turned it over. "Is this your card?"

Scarlet's eyes lit up. "It is. How did you do that?"

"That's remarkable," James gushed.

"You're a magician, I see," Emma said.

Rig took the cards and put them all together. "Over the years I learned a few things. I got into card tricks when I was young. I spent a considerable amount of time indoors and by myself."

"Well, it appears that time spent paid off," Emma said.

"After what happened to me, I didn't want to be with others. I thought doing card tricks was a way for me to impress people, considering my other setbacks."

"Can you teach me?" Scarlet asked.

"They say a magician doesn't share his secrets," Rig teased.

"Oh, please," Scarlet pleaded.

"For you I'll make an exception," Rig said.

Emma looked at the clock and said, "Not tonight though, time for you to go to bed. Head upstairs and get ready."

"Five more minutes, please," Scarlet begged.

"No. Now say thank you to Rig for showing you those tricks," Emma said, getting to her feet and walking over to Scarlet.

"Thank you," Scarlet said. She got up, went to Rig, and gave him a hug. "Good night."

"Good night, Miss Scarlet."

Taking Emma's hand, the two went upstairs.

James got to his feet, went to a tray nearby, and opened a decanter of brandy. "Do you want a glass?"

"Sure," Rig said.

James returned with two glasses. He handed one to Rig and sat down in the chair next to him.

"Thank you for your hospitality," Rig said.

"No, I need to be thanking you, but…" James said. He paused to collect his thoughts.

"You're curious as to why I'm here, why I'm helping you," Rig said, already knowing what was vexing James.

"Out of nowhere you appeared yesterday and saved me. Why?"

"If I tell you everything, you won't believe it."

"How about giving me the benefit of the doubt."

Rig took a sip of the brandy and said, "Very well, but I won't be surprised if you find my story to be fanciful."

"The floor is yours," James said. "And it should be noted that after the week I've had, I wouldn't be shocked by anything anymore."

"I grew up in Connecticut…"

"So it will be a long story, I see," James quipped.

"It will; to tell it without context would be even more confusing."

"Go ahead. I apologize for interrupting you."

Rig looked at the flickering flames of the fire, the glow reflecting off his face. "I can't say I had a normal childhood. I grew up in a well-to-do family back in Connecticut. My father owned a brokerage that dealt in shipping. He had offices in New York, Boston and Philadelphia. He often was gone, leaving me in the care of nannies, which I was fine with. I didn't mind him being gone so much. You see, my mother had died giving birth to me, and he liked to remind me of that any time he had more than a couple of drinks.

"Outside of nannies and tutors, I was like any other child. I enjoyed games and playing outside, but I had few friends. One day I went into town with one of my nannies; I was eleven, by the way. I saw a group of children my age playing at a park. While my nanny went inside a shop, I snuck away and went to see what the other children were doing. They befriended me almost instantly; it was something opposite of what my father said of people. You see, he didn't like people much and many times would declare that you couldn't trust anyone. Well, I found this not to be the case. When my nanny found me later, she scolded me and dragged me off. I swore though that I'd return and play again. It was the first time I had people in my life whom I could connect with.

"Weeks went by and I longed to go see them. I asked my nanny if I could go, but she refused. I then took it upon myself. I went to the barn, was getting a horse ready, and that's when my life changed forever. A feral dog appeared in the barn. It spooked the horses, and before I knew it, a lantern that was on the wall was knocked off. The barn exploded into flames, further inciting the horses. I was knocked down and that's all I remember. When I awoke, I was bandaged from the left side of my face down to my left hip. A groundskeeper saved me."

"I'm truly sorry," James said, his mind racing to the one night he'd set the cabin on fire. He could see the boy and the flames sticking to him like glue. He shook away the dark thought and said, "What did your father say?"

"My father came home and didn't say much. They asked me why I was down in the barn, but I lied, said I heard something. Thing is, it didn't matter. I would never be the same person, and with my face looking like it did, the last thing I wanted to do was see anyone else. The irony was I wanted friends and to be around people, but in my haste to have it, I destroyed any real chance. Then it happened…" Rig said, pausing to take a drink.

Intrigued by what he meant, James leaned forward.

"I can still remember the dream, if you want to call it that. I woke in a terrible sweat and had a sense of dread. What's odd is the dread didn't pertain to me, but to someone else. I could see them in my mind's eye as if it were more a memory though I'd never met this person. The dream was followed by an urge, a burning desire to do something about it, but I couldn't, I was only eleven. The desire waned but was replaced by another dream. This time it was a different person; they too needed help. This went on for years. I'd have the dark dreams, that's what I call them, and I'd see these people. I didn't do anything, and like I said, the desire to help would eventually go away.

"When I was nineteen, my father passed away and left me with the family fortune. The night after his last will and testament was read to me, I had one of those dark dreams. This time I woke and decided I would find this person. I set out the next day. I traveled to a small town in Maine; there I found the person, a woman. She'd been raped, but the law in town wouldn't hear her case. I found the man responsible and took justice into my own hands."

"You killed him?" James asked.

"No, it's not like that. It's as if I'm being given these visions for a variety of reasons. First I'm being called upon by God or something mystical to find these victims and help them. When I happen upon the perpetrators, I don't go in seeking to kill them but to save them from evil ways. I give them a chance at redemption. The thing is most don't take it; in fact, many try to kill me, which leaves me no option but to defend myself."

"You really are some sort of guardian angel, then," James said.

"I don't know what you'd call it, but this is now my life. I have a vast fortune that I never wanted, so I put it to good use by helping all who seek it."

"And you had one of these dreams about me?" James asked.

"No, my dream was about Scarlet. I woke and could see her praying for help," Rig answered.

James sat back and chuckled.

"Did I say something humorous?" Rig asked.

"No, on the contrary. When this ordeal with John and Cecil began, the men came to the house and Scarlet met them. She knew I was in trouble, so she went and prayed. She told Emma and me that a guardian angel was coming to save us. So you see, you are an answer to her prayers; you are her...our guardian angel."

"Again, I wouldn't say that."

"Thank you for helping us," James said.

"It's not over yet. John and Cecil have to be dealt with," Rig said before taking a drink.

"I wouldn't presume to know how to handle this, so

if you have a plan, I'd love to hear it."

"I'm going to talk with them, probably tomorrow."

"And?"

"I'll try to persuade them," Rig answered. "Let me ask you, is leaving an option for you and your family?"

"No, we're not leaving. I've built too much to just give it up," James declared. He got up and filled his glass.

"Then I'll have to reason with John to leave town and abandon any plans to harm you."

James let out a loud laugh. "Good luck."

"Mr. Harris, I don't believe in luck."

"Then how do you explain what you did yesterday? I saw how it ended. How did you manage to shoot down four men without getting a scratch?" James asked.

"I have the good fortune of knowing when I'll die. It's one of the dark dreams I have often, and I can tell you that I wasn't meant to die in that restaurant yesterday."

"Then I should breathe a sigh of relief because you'll succeed in your dealings with John?"

Rig finished his drink and got up to pour himself more. Taking the decanter, he replied, "I wouldn't say that."

"But you just said that you've already seen how you die. Can I assume it's not by the hands of John or his men?"

"It is not."

"Then I have to conclude you'll be successful against them," James said.

"I will prevail, of that I have no doubt, but the detail you're missing is will you survive?" Rig replied bluntly.

"I'm confused," James said, alarmed by Rig's answer.

"I have these dreams; they show me the people who are suffering. Sometimes I'm able to save the people, but there have been occasions where I don't. Justice always comes to those men, but sometimes the innocent die in the crossfire, you could say."

"Then you're not a guardian angel," James said.

"I never said I was. I'm a man who has a gift. I use it to try to bring justice to those who can't get it, nothing more. Sometimes things get violent and there's bloodshed, but one thing is always certain, justice is always served."

"What should I do, then?"

"I suggest you stay clear of town, keep your family in the house, and let me do what I do. If you involve yourself, you're liable to get hurt or, worse, get your family hurt," Rig advised.

"Just sit and wait?" James asked. "I can't just do nothing."

"You're more than welcome to go about your day as you see fit, but I can't be everywhere all the time," Rig said, drinking the glass of brandy down with a single gulp. "I do suggest you keep your family sequestered though, maybe even hire some of your workers to guard them."

"I don't know what to say," James said, his hands trembling. "You think they'll strike out at my family?"

"There's a good chance. Once I make my intentions clear to them, things tend to go sideways."

"Then we'll be prepared. I'll do as you say."

Rig returned to his chair and said, "I've never told anyone my story before. I don't know why I shared it with you, but I did. Know this, Mr. Harris, I will do everything in my power to ensure you and your family are safe, but you need to stay clear of town."

"That I can do."

"Good."

"Why do you have them repent?" James asked, curious as to that specific detail.

"I've never been told that I had to have them do so, it's just something that has felt natural to do. I give them a chance, one last time, at redemption; they then make the choice."

"Can I share something with you?" James asked.

"Sure."

"When I first saw you, and your…face, I thought you were a ghost or something."

"A ghost?"

"I'll just tell you the truth, I've been doing a lot of that lately," James said, shifting in his chair. He cleared his throat and detailed to Rig the story of how he knew John and Cecil, how he'd killed those people, and why they were now here in town.

Finishing, James said, "That's why when I saw you, I thought that maybe you were the ghost of the boy I had killed those many years ago."

"I'm no ghost, Mr. Harris, but I'm sad to hear what happened to those people."

"I'm more saddened by my actions than anybody, and now I'm reaping those sins I committed. I'm filled with regret for what I did and have asked God's forgiveness; I just don't know if he's listened to my prayer."

Rig leaned in close to James and said, "God has forgiven you. You must now forgive yourself and lead a life to prove you're worthy."

"I've been trying to," James confessed.

"Good, just wake every day with renewed purpose to do that, but please know that you've been forgiven."

James raised his brow and said, "You're the most interesting person I've ever met. I'll admit that your appearance was much to take in, and it's one of the reasons Emma was taken aback upon seeing you, but now I know that was my own prejudice. One must never judge a book by its cover."

"No, they shouldn't, Mr. Harris; no, they shouldn't," Rig said.

Loud knocking came from the front door.

James and Rig gave each other a concerned look.

Getting up, James said, "It might be Christopher."

"Or it may not be," Rig said, standing tall and pulling out his pistol. "Let me answer the door."

"Very well."

"Stay here," Rig said and moved to the front door. He pulled the drape aside and saw a man he'd never met before.

"Who is it?" James asked from the parlor.

"A short man with a thick gray beard."

"It's Cecil," James said.

"Well, never a better time to meet him," Rig said, unlocking the door and opening it. "Hi, Cecil."

Shocked to see it was Rig, Cecil took a step back and said, "You?"

"If you're wishing to see—"

"I'm here to see you," Cecil said.

"How can I be of service?"

"Mr. Kemp wishes to meet with you, say tomorrow morning around nine at his office in town."

"I'll be there," Rig said and went to close the door.

"How did you do it?" Cecil asked abruptly.

Rig hesitated from closing the door and asked, "Do what?"

"Beat our men like you did, then kill them all without getting hurt?"

"Like a magician, I never tell my secrets. Tell Mr. Kemp I'll see him tomorrow at nine," Rig said and slammed the door.

"So tomorrow it ends?" James asked.

"We shall see," Rig said. "Thank you for the drink and the good chat. I'll be retiring for the night."

"Good night," James said.

Rig disappeared down the hall.

James poured himself one more drink and sat in front of the fire. He prayed for Rig's success at tomorrow's meeting and added to his prayer that he would see the end of John Kemp and Cecil Brangan.

CHAPTER ELEVEN

OCTOBER 2, 1876

MENTRYVILLE, CALIFORNIA

Fire nudged Rig with his head as he hitched him outside Garcia's old office building.

"You're worried?" Rig asked Fire as he petted his neck. "You don't need to be, I'll be fine."

Fire whined and rubbed his head once more against Rig.

"It will be fine," Rig said. He couldn't read Fire's mind but he had a sense of what the horse was always thinking. The two had been together for years and Rig had come to love the horse as if he was his own child.

"Time to go inside and take care of business," Rig said to Fire. He stepped onto the walkway then remembered that Scarlet had given him a note. He pulled it out of his pocket and unfolded it.

It read, *"Stay safe and thank you."*

Her message warmed his heart. He was a man so

used to being stigmatized for his appearance that when someone acted in a contrarian way, it showed him that mankind was redeemable.

Ready to tackle what laid ahead, he stepped into the office to find Cecil standing there waiting for him, his arms folded and a smirk on his face.

"You're here and on time," Cecil snarked.

"I'm very punctual," Rig said, removing his hat.

Hearing him from the back office, John emerged. "I would say you are a very punctual man, seeing that you showed up to save James Harris at the right time."

"My timing can be impeccable," Rig said.

"Mr.?" John asked.

"Call me Rig."

"Mr. Rig?" John asked.

"No, just Rig."

"Don't you have a last name, or is that it?" John asked.

"Like I said, Rig is fine."

"Very well, this way," John said, motioning for Rig to come into his office.

Rig obliged and entered.

John turned to Cecil and said, "You can join us."

Cecil nodded and followed John inside.

Taking a seat at the desk once occupied by Garcia, John got right to business. "I'm here to make a deal with you."

"And what would that be?" Rig asked. He was always curious about such things. If he could avoid bloodshed by way of striking a compromise that was suitable, he would consider taking it.

"Whatever James is paying you, I'll double it," John said.

"I don't think so," Rig said.

John sighed and said, "Fine, I'll triple it, but that's it."

"I'm afraid the answer is no."

"Is there something wrong with my money?" John asked, his tone showing a tinge of frustration.

"Actually, there is something wrong with your money, and that is, it isn't yours to begin with. I know you stole it, and second, Mr. Harris isn't paying me."

"He isn't?"

"No, he's not."

"Then however he's compensating you, I'll do better," John said.

Cecil grunted slightly upon hearing John negotiate in such a way with Rig.

"He's not compensating me in any way," Rig said.

"I'm confused. Then why are you helping him?" John asked.

"I'm not just helping him, I'm also helping the family."

"And for what? He must be paying you handsomely. You're without a doubt a talented fighter, having bested my men twice and killed the likes of Franklin Ashe."

"Was he the man I shot in the head yesterday?" Rig mocked.

"He was," Cecil barked in a seething tone from behind Rig.

John shot Cecil a hard stare, signaling he wanted him to remain quiet.

"I've never heard of Franklin Ashe and only met him for the first time the other day," Rig said.

"Why are you helping James?" John asked.

"I'm helping them on account they need help defending against the likes of you and your men; that's why. I'm not a hired gun or whatever you think I am."

"But he hired you, no?"

"No, he didn't. I knew he was in need, so I came," Rig said, giving as much detail as he would to John.

John leaned back in his chair. A smile stretched across his face. "You're telling me that you go around helping random people, and that James here just happened to be one of those chance encounters?"

"I didn't say that it was random, I just said I'm here to help and he didn't hire me or send for me."

"You're confusing me, and you know something, I don't care. What I want to know is what's your price? How much to get you to work for me?"

"There's nothing you could give me to ever work for you, Mr. Kemp. However, I have an offer for you," Rig said.

"You have an offer for me." John chuckled.

"You and your men pack up and leave town, but before you go, you'll need to sign over that piece of land to Mr. Harris and his partner, Christopher Sheer."

John scrunched his face and gave Rig a perplexed look. "Are you serious?"

"I am. I'll also ask that you repent for your sins too."

"So let me understand this offer. I repent, give my land to James and his partner, then leave town?"

"Yes, that's correct."

"And what if I don't?" John asked.

"Then I'll be compelled to force you to leave."

John burst out into laughter followed by Cecil.

Slapping his hand on the desk as he laughed, John said, "That's some offer. So you alone will compel me, did I hear that right?"

"Yes."

"Son, do you not know who I am?"

"I do know who you are. You're John Kemp of Kemp's Raiders out of Missouri. You're known for committing war crimes, murder, rape, pillaging, theft and more; you served nine years in a Missouri state penitentiary before coming west. However, before you arrived, you and your partner back there robbed banks and stole the money you've now used to buy land and influence in town."

"I see you do know me," John said, not sure if he should be impressed or concerned by Rig knowing his biography.

"Mr. Kemp, it's very easy, just repent, give the land back to Mr. Harris and Mr. Sheer, pay back the money you stole, then leave. If you do so, I'll leave you alone."

"Do you believe this?" John asked Cecil as he pointed at Rig. "He's saying he'll leave us alone."

"Want me to end this right now?" Cecil asked, moving his right hand back to his pistol that hung snugly on his hip.

"Don't do that, Mr. Brangan," Rig said even though he couldn't see Cecil moving towards his pistol.

John waved off Cecil and said, "Let us have some

privacy."

"Are you sure?" Cecil asked.

"Don't make me ask twice," John said to Cecil.

Annoyed and angered by his dismissal, Cecil got up and exited the office, slamming the door behind him.

"Mr. Rig, there has to be some accommodation or agreement we can come to. Just tell me—anything. I'm sure a man like you could use some extra money or women; how about I hire you some women?" John said.

"I have plenty of money and a woman who is waiting for me. Let's get back to my offer to you."

"What you're proposing isn't going to occur, that's a simple fact. The only way I'm getting dislodged from this town and the opportunity that's here for me is by way of the undertaker," John declared.

Rig stood and said, "I'm sorry to hear that." He turned and headed for the door.

"That's it, you're leaving?"

"Yes, you gave me your answer. Now I have to leave and prepare."

Again John burst out into laughter. "We're not done; we're negotiating here."

"Mr. Kemp, I don't need anything you're offering, so I don't see how we'll come to any arrangement."

"Can I assume then that you're an adversary of mine?"

"Yes, you can."

"Then you leave me no choice but to confront you at a time and place of my choosing," John threatened.

Taking his hat, Rig said, "Do what you must, Mr. Kemp; but know that I gave you a choice, and you opted out. Now if you'll excuse me, I have some biscuits and gravy waiting for me at Ruthie's." Rig turned and exited the office.

Cecil came in and closed the door. "What happened?"

"Gather the men," John said, his temper on the verge of flaring.

"I like the sound of that. Might I ask what's about to happen?" Cecil asked.

John stood and said, "We're going to war."

"Oh boy, this is going to be fun," Cecil said as he raced out of the office.

***

James told Emma everything Rig had divulged to him, leaving her more frightened than she had ever been. "Should we leave, James?"

"I've told you before, you can leave, but I'm staying. What message do I send my people if I pack up and leave?"

"It shows you're sane, that's what," she barked.

"No, it shows I'm a coward. It's one thing to remain at home, another to up and leave town. We'll do what he suggested and stay at the house. Let him do what he needs to do; then all should be back to normal."

"But what if Rig isn't successful?"

"I don't think we have to worry about that. We just need to keep our heads down for a few days."

"Mama, why are you and Papa fighting?" Scarlet asked from the open doorway.

"Sweetheart, everything is fine," Emma replied.

"It doesn't sound like it," Scarlet said.

"Come here," Emma said, her arms open wide.

Scarlet scurried across the creaking floor and hopped into Emma's arms.

James looked at them. His heart ached, as he did have concern for their safety, yet he was having a hard time letting them go. Rig's words came crashing back to him. "I'm going to put you on the first coach to Los Angeles. I'll have you stay at a hotel there until this clears up."

"Los Angeles?"

"It's the closest town. That way when this is all over, you can be here in a day's travel," James said.

With the opportunity to leave, Emma sat and thought.

"Mama, I don't want to leave Papa. We can't," Scarlet said.

"But it's not safe here anymore," Emma softly replied.

"We have Rig. He'll keep us safe," Scarlet countered.

"I'm not sure he can. He explained to—" Emma said before being cut off by James.

"It's just an extra layer of caution is all," James said to Scarlet.

Knowing why James interrupted her, Emma said, "We wouldn't be gone for too long."

"But, Mama, this is our home. We Harrises don't run from trouble, we stand up for ourselves. Isn't that what you've taught me? It's why I didn't take stuff from that boy at school," Scarlet said passionately.

Hearing their own words, both James and Emma

stared at her, unsure how to reply.

"I agree that we don't run from trouble, but right now this is different," Emma explained.

"How so?" Scarlet asked.

Emma wanted to just tell her that John could possibly resort to murder but didn't want to frighten her too much.

"Mama, I don't want to go," Scarlet whimpered. "We need to stay and be here for Papa and Rig."

"James, help me here," Emma said, her eyes pleading for James to just make the decision for them.

Filled with pride that Scarlet wanted to stand tall and not cower, his mind went to how he'd acted when pressed eleven years ago. He couldn't help but see the contrast.

"We're staying, all of us," James said.

"Are you sure?" Emma asked.

"Yes, we'll be safe as long as we stay at the house. But to make you feel better, I'll get Aaron and some others from the well to come guard the house," James said.

"Fine, just get them here as soon as you can," Emma said.

"I'll head out now," James said.

"But it's dark out. Are you certain?" Emma asked.

"What is the dark, Scarlet?" James asked.

"Darkness is just the absence of light," Scarlet replied.

"Exactly, which means no one will see me," James said. He got on his knees so he was eye level with Scarlet and took her hand. Gently caressing it, he said, "Have I told you how proud I am of you lately?"

She shook her head.

"Well, I am, you're not just a beautiful little girl, but more importantly you're smart and brave; those are excellent traits and gifts to have."

Scarlet blushed.

"What do you say to Papa for the compliment?" Emma nudged.

"Thank you," Scarlet said.

"I also want to thank you," James said.

"For what?" Scarlet asked.

"Your faith and prayers have given us Rig, and he has truly been a godsend," James said.

"He is our guardian angel, isn't he?" she asked.

"He is, he truly is," James said.

CHAPTER TWELVE

OCTOBER 3, 1876

MENTRYVILLE, CALIFORNIA

Pulling the drapes aside, James peered out the second-story window and down on the front yard of the house. There he spotted George, one of the men Aaron had sent to guard the house. In George's hands was a Winchester rifle.

The sky was covered in dark gray clouds, and a heavy breeze whisked dry leaves across the yard. "A storm is coming," James said.

"I should get the clothes off the line," Emma said as she finished making the bed.

"I'm going to head downstairs and talk with Rig," James said. He exited the room, went down the hall and down the narrow stairs.

Rig was in the kitchen, making himself breakfast.

James walked in and said, "Let Emma take care of that."

"I wouldn't hear of it. Plus I already have a helper," Rig said, flipping an egg on the cast-iron pan.

Scarlet emerged from the back door, holding her apron. "Brrr, it's getting cold outside."

"Where have you been?" James asked.

"Getting some eggs. I need to run back and get the rest," Scarlet said, carefully taking what she had from her apron.

James peered through the glass on the door and scanned the backyard.

With the handful of eggs on the counter, Scarlet rushed to the door and said, "I'll be right back."

"Okay," Rig said.

Noticing he didn't see the second man, James went to the front of the house and spotted George again. He opened the door and asked, "Where's Michael?"

"Hey, boss, he's around back. I think he set up near the shed," George hollered.

"We're making breakfast. I'll bring you out some eggs and bread shortly."

"Thank you, boss."

Seeing George was shivering, James said, "I'll also bring you an overcoat too."

"Much obliged, it's getting chilly," George said, stamping his feet.

James again looked to the sky. The cloud cover was thicker and darker. Soon the storm would be upon them. He closed the door just as he heard a scream from the backyard. He raced through the house and to the back door, only to find Rig standing there.

Scarlet sprinted towards them. "He's dead, he's dead!"

Rig pulled his pistol and cocked it. He raced towards Scarlet, meeting her halfway, and scooped her up with his left arm.

Emma appeared in the kitchen, frantic. "What's going on? Where's Scarlet? I heard a scream."

Rig leapt onto the back porch from the yard, easily clearing four feet and through the back door.

With them safely inside, James slammed the door shut and locked it.

"He's dead, he's dead," Scarlet wailed.

Wiping her hair from her face, Rig asked, "Who's dead? What did you see?"

"The man…the man Papa hired to guard us is dead," Scarlet answered, her breathing rapid.

Emma covered her mouth with her hand and gasped.

"Are you sure?" Rig asked.

Scarlet nodded her head quickly, her eyes wide with fear.

Rig raced from the kitchen and into the parlor, where he had his rifle propped up against the wall. He took it and ran back. "Do you have any weapons in the house?"

Shaking his head, James answered, "No."

"Take this," Rig said, holding out the rifle.

James stared at the Model 1876 Winchester.

"Are you going to help me protect your family or not?" Rig asked.

James shook off his hesitation and grabbed the

rifle.

"One is already in the chamber. Just cock the hammer back," Rig said. He went to the kitchen window and peered out. He scanned the backyard but didn't see anyone.

A gunshot sounded from out front.

"George," James yelped. He ran to the front and looked out the window to see George lying on the ground. It appeared he was still alive.

In the kitchen, Rig said to Emma, "Take Scarlet and go upstairs."

Filled with terror, Emma did as he said without uttering a word. She got Scarlet to her feet, and the two went directly up to the master bedroom and closed the door.

Rig went to the front and asked, "What happened?"

"It's George. I think he's been shot," James replied.

Pulling the blinds back, Rig looked and saw George crawling towards the house. "Cover me."

"Where are you going?" James asked.

"To save him," Rig said, his pistol cocked and ready in his hand. He threw open the door and ran outside.

James put the rifle to his shoulder and aimed out. He pivoted the muzzle back and forth, unsure where to aim.

Rig made it to George, only to find him dead. "Rest in peace, brother," he said. He picked up George's rifle and removed his pistol from his belt then raced back to the house. As he jumped onto the porch, a gunshot cracked. The post next to his head exploded, with wood chips flying around him.

James swung the rifle in the direction he heard the gunfire and pulled the trigger. The .45-75-caliber round exploded from the barrel and whizzed by a group of John's men crouching in the distance.

Rig jumped across the threshold, followed by James. Rig slammed the door shut and said, "Go to the back and make sure no one is coming."

James nodded and ran to the back just in time. He spotted a man holding a bottle; a cloth dangled from it on fire. James cycled the lever action, aimed and pulled the trigger. This time the round exited, smashed through the window, and struck the man dead center in the chest. He dropped to his knees and fell over, the bottle hitting the ground without doing any damage. "I got one."

"Good man, now stay there. They'll be coming, I imagine in waves," Rig barked.

"Okay," James said.

Minutes passed without any other encounter. It began to feel as if the attack had passed.

"Where are they?" James asked. His hands gripped the rifle tightly.

"Be patient. They're just probing," Rig said.

In the distance near the chicken coop, James spotted movement. He looked more closely and saw two men. Not waiting for them to attack him, he put the butt of the rifle in his shoulder and raised it. Looking down the barrel, he placed the first man he saw in the sights, placed his finger on the trigger, and began to squeeze. The rifle fired. The bullet blasted through the already smashed window and struck its target in the face. The man reeled back and disappeared out of sight. "I got him. I got another one!" James howled in joy. He lowered the rifle and thought about his celebratory response. After the events in Missouri eleven years ago, he had forgone using weapons and hadn't fired one since then. Now here he was defending his family and finding enjoyment in doing so at the same time.

From upstairs, Emma screamed, "They're coming from the side. They have torches!"

The word *torches* conjured up images from the night in Missouri. He raced from the kitchen to a window in the dining room that looked out to the side. When he arrived, he saw two men sprinting with torches in their hands. He smashed the window with the butt of the rifle, cycled the lever, and took aim on the closest man. He steadied his breathing and fired, but missed the man. "Argh!" he spat.

Rig appeared next to him, his rifle at the ready. Not wasting a second, Rig fired, cycled his rifle, and fired again. Both shots hit their intended targets, sending both men to the ground dead.

"Good shooting," James chirped.

"We're not out of the woods yet," Rig said. "If they get one of those torches into the house...well, you know what will happen."

"I'm quite aware," James said.

"I'm falling back to the front of the house," Rig said, cocking the lever of the rifle just before he turned and left.

James peered through the shattered window and looked at the bodies on the ground, the torches flickering.

Rain began to fall; the heavy drops hit the metal roof. Soon the sky ripped open and a downpour ensued.

The torches that lay on the ground soon were extinguished.

When James first heard the crack, he wondered if it was thunder. He looked to the sky for lightning but saw none; then a round whizzed by his head and struck the wall behind him. He dropped to the floor and took cover. Within seconds a barrage of gunfire erupted from all sides of the house.

"Everyone get down!" Rig hollered.

The heavy and endless volley of bullets shredded the walls, furniture, and anything in its way.

With his knees curled up to his chest, James sat praying he or his family wouldn't get hit.

The gunfire ended just as quickly as it had started.

James looked around at the debris strewn around the dining room caused by the heavy barrage.

An explosive sound of wood and glass came from the kitchen.

James knew it had to be someone coming inside. Though fear gripped him, he knew he had to act. He sprang to his feet, chambered a round, and aimed it at the door that separated him from the kitchen.

The door slowly creaked open.

That was enough for James. He pulled the trigger, cycled the lever, and fired again.

A loud thump sounded on the other side along with a grunt. "I'm shot," a man wailed.

Gunfire then came from the front room. It had to be Rig engaging targets.

Without warning, bullets ripped through the dining room door, just missing James. He ducked and took cover behind a sideboard.

In the front room, Rig was firing upon six men who were running towards the front of the house. The man leading them was Billy. He had fired twice, taking two of them down, cycled the lever, and found the rifle empty. He tossed it on the floor, pulled his Colt, cocked it and aimed just as a man breached the front door. He fired, hitting the man in the side of the neck. He cocked the Colt again, but before he could get a shot off, a bullet ripped through his left shoulder. He paused for a brief second, looked at the bloody hole in his jacket, and mused that this was the first time he'd ever been shot.

The man on the ground took aim and fired. The round struck Rig in the leg.

Rig dropped to one knee. Now he'd been hit twice. Something wasn't right; this wasn't how he was supposed to die…he thought. He didn't hesitate, aimed and killed the man on the floor with a shot through the head.

Billy and two other men came in through the front door. Billy stumbled over the dead body and fell to the floor. The other two looked around the dimly lit space and spotted Rig. They turned, but Rig unloaded his pistol into them both. With his pistol empty and no time to reload, he pulled his knife from the sheath on his hip and lunged at

Billy on the floor. He straddled him quickly and plunged the blade deep into his chest and twisted.

Billy gasped, blood spurting from his mouth. He stared into Rig's eyes and tried to plead, but it was too late.

Rig removed the blade and plunged it once more to ensure Billy was dead.

Hearing the commotion in the front, James crawled his way to the door that separated the dining room from the hall. He opened it, peeked through and saw Rig on top of a man. He then spotted a man he recognized from the fight outside the lumberyard. It was Roger and he was coming towards the front door with his pistol raised. James quickly acted, put the rifle to his shoulder and fired. This time his aim was true, striking Roger in the center of his chest, dropping him where he stood.

Rig looked towards James with a look of shock, then to the open doorway, to see the man sprawled out on the ground just inches from the porch stairs.

The dining room door burst open and in came Samuel. Seeing James on the floor, he fired, hitting him in the hip.

James cried out in pain and rolled over, but when he pulled the trigger, nothing happened because he hadn't reloaded the rifle. Frozen, he simply stared at Samuel, who stood over him, smiling, his barrel leveled at his face. Was this it? he thought.

"Say goodbye," Samuel said. He cocked his pistol, but before he could shoot, Rig reacted with speed and decisiveness. He picked up Billy's pistol, cocked it, and rapidly fired two rounds at Samuel, both smashing into his chest. Samuel gasped, dropped the pistol, and fell to the floor dead.

James grimaced in pain as he pulled himself into a sitting position. He placed his trembling hand on the exit wound in his hip and was grateful that it had gone clean through.

"How you doing?" Rig asked as he scurried clear of the open doorway for cover.

"I'm hit. Got shot in the hip," James replied.

"Me too, shoulder and leg," Rig said. "Any idea how many men Kemp has?"

"No."

A voice bellowed from outside, "Give it up, James!"

"It's him," James said to Rig.

"This is where he tries to negotiate for you to come out. Don't think about it," Rig said as he ripped open his trousers to examine the wound in his thigh.

"I'm not going outside, believe me. I don't have a death wish," James said.

"James, this is just the beginning," John barked.

"He's lying. If he had more men, he'd send them in. I think we've taken a hefty toll on him," Rig said. He tore a piece of his shirt off and wrapped it around the wound to stop it from bleeding. "Say, how's your wound?"

"Hurts, but I'll live," James replied.

"Can you move or walk?" Rig asked.

"Not sure," James said. He pushed against the wall and inch by inch slowly got to his feet. When he put weight on the side that was hit, a spike of pain shot through his body. "I don't think I'm going to be able to walk too well."

"Try," Rig shouted. He finished bandaging his leg and stood. The wound hurt, but he was able to walk.

James took a step, but the pain was too much, causing him to drop to his knees. "I can't. I think the bullet might have chipped the bone or something worse."

"I'll come to you," Rig said. He slowly made his way, stepping over debris. He reached James and helped him sit up, his back against the wall again. Seeing a napkin on the table, he took it and pressed it against the wound. "Hold this."

James did as he said, "Do you think they'll attack again?"

"They might, so we need to hurry up and get ourselves bandaged up and reloaded," Rig said as he tore a strip from the tablecloth and wrapped it over the napkin on James' hip. "This will help slow the bleeding."

"James, come on out!" John hollered again.

"I'm not coming out. You come here and we can talk!" James replied.

Scarlet appeared in the doorway, covered in blood.

Seeing her, James' stomach tightened. "Scarlet, have you been shot?"

"It's Mama," Scarlet wept.

James tried to get to his feet, but the pain was immense.

"I'll go," Rig said.

"Take her with you," James ordered.

Rig picked Scarlet up with his good arm and carried her up the stairs. Each step he took shot jolts of pain through his leg, but he overcame it. Reaching the master bedroom, he found Emma lying on the floor, clutching her upper arm. He went to her side and asked, "Where are you hit?"

"Just in my arm. I'll be fine," Emma said.

Scarlet sat next to Emma and wrapped her arms around her. "I'm scared."

Rig took a pillow from the bed, removed the case and wrapped it over her arm. "The wound looks clean. I'll examine it later, okay?"

"Is it over?" Emma asked.

"I don't think so," Rig said.

"James, I'm giving you one last chance to surrender or I'll go in there and kill everyone, do you hear me?" John shouted.

"What should we do?" Emma asked.

"I think he's bluffing. We've killed many of his men; rough count is about ten or so," Rig said.

"I pray you're right," Emma said. She then noticed Rig's wounds and said, "You've been shot...twice."

"I'll be fine," Rig said. He tied a knot in the pillowcase and checked to make sure it was snug on her arm. He reached into his jacket and pulled out a Remington Model 95 double-barreled derringer. He handed it to her and said, "Take this."

Emma didn't hesitate taking the pistol. "Do I just pull back on this?" she asked, referring to the hammer.

"Yes, it fires once and that's it, so use it wisely."

"Thank you."

"You're welcome," Rig said and went to get up.

She grabbed his arm, stopping him. "Will you forgive me for how I first treated you?"

"There's nothing to forgive. Now I must go."

Outside, John looked at Cecil, his eyes showing the concern that ran through his mind.

"What do we do?" Cecil asked, the rain spilling off his brim.

"We try to get him to come out; then we kill him," John said.

"But, John, they've killed all of our men," Cecil said, fear emanating in his tone.

Ever persistent, John called out, "James, I'm giving you this one last chance. Come out, surrender, and I'll spare your family."

Inside the house, James ran through the number that had been killed. It was a lot, enough to fill him with confidence that they'd just about killed all of John's men. He crawled to the window, each inch sending painful reminders of the wound in his hip. He pulled himself up next to the open window and shouted, "If you want me, you'll have to come get me. Now come on, you coward, come kill me!"

Rig appeared next to him. "Emma is fine, just a flesh wound in the arm."

"Thank God," James said with a sigh.

Cecil turned to John and said, "What do we do?"

Frustrated, John conceded defeat and said, "Let's go back to the office, get our things and go."

"We're not just leaving here, we're leaving town?" Cecil asked, shocked by the answer.

"I don't know who that man he has in there is, but he's now bested us three times. We go back, get what money we have left, and leave. We might have lost this battle, but we'll win the war, believe me," John said with a reassuring tone.

"I'm with you, always have been," Cecil said.

The two stood up from behind a rock and hurried away.

Seeing John and Cecil retreat, James said, "They're leaving. I only see John and Cecil."

Rig finished reloading his Colt, holstered it, and picked up Samuel's pistol and shoved it into his belt. He turned and headed for the door.

"Where are you going?" James asked.

"I'm putting an end to this right now," Rig answered. He stepped over the bodies piled in the entry and out into the pouring rain.

James called after him, "I'm not letting you go alone!"

Rig ignored him. He went to the small barn, got Fire, and saddled him.

Determined, James got himself to his feet and shuffled, using the wall to help support him. He made it to the foyer and stopped when he came upon the bodies.

From the top of the stairs, Emma asked, "Is it over?"

"The attack is over, but Rig just left to go confront John and Cecil. I need to go help him," James said.

Emma came down the stairs and saw that James had been shot. "But you're injured."

"Emma, I need to help him. I can't let him risk going alone," James said.

"But he'll be fine, I'm sure of it," Emma said, fearful that if James went, he might not return.

"No, I'm going. Now help me to the door," he insisted.

"You can't be of help if you can't even walk," Emma said, pointing out the obvious.

James pressed his eyes closed and shifted his right leg. The pain was excruciating, yet he managed. He did it several more times and made it past the bodies and to the open door.

Rig and Fire bolted from the barn.

"Stop!" James hollered.

Not paying James any attention, Rig rode past and down the drive.

Undeterred, James hopped down the stairs, stopping at the bottom. He looked at the twenty yards to the barn. The rain was coming down heavy and there was nothing to support his weight or support him. He glanced around and saw a flat-head shovel near a flower bed. He jumped over, took the grip-handled shovel, and propped it under his armpit like a crutch. Using every ounce of strength and willpower, he cleared the distance to the barn. Inside, he paused to catch his breath. Looking around, he now saw that he'd have to saddle the horse, which seemed daunting, but he wasn't going to allow Rig to take John on alone.

He made it to the saddle, put the shovel down, and grasped it. He went to pick it up, but the weight was too much for his hip, causing him to fall backwards. "Argh!" he hollered. He sat up and went to push the saddle off him when Emma appeared and lifted it up. "Your arm," he said.

"If you're going to go, then you need to go now," she said, walking the saddle over to the horse and throwing it on its back. She fastened it as best she could with her one arm bandaged and went back to help him up.

Back on his feet, James hobbled over to the horse and, with Emma's help, got on its back. "Thank you," he said.

"Here," she said, handing him a Colt New Army she'd found on the floor in the house.

He went to inspect it to make sure it was loaded, but she stopped him. "It's ready to shoot. Now go, hurry."

"I love you," he said.

"Go," she said and slapped the hindquarters of the horse.

***

"Hurry, put everything in the crate!" John barked at Cecil as he walked back into the office.

"I'm moving as fast as I can," Cecil replied as he hastily grabbed the coin and cash from the safe located in a back room.

John rolled up plat maps and gathered all the documents and deeds he had acquired for every parcel and lot of land he now owned in and around town.

The door to the office opened and in stepped Rig, his clothes dripping wet. In his hand he held his Colt Buntline, the hammer back. "Put everything down and put your hands up."

John did as Rig ordered.

Cecil was crouched down in front of the safe and heard Rig command John. He stopped what he was doing and pulled his pistol from its holster.

"Where's your partner?" Rig asked.

"He's not here," John lied.

"If you're here, don't think about doing anything, do you hear me," Rig shouted for Cecil to hear.

"What do you want?" John asked.

"I'll get to that," Rig replied. "Where's your partner?"

"I said he's not here. He's at the barn getting some things for our departure."

"You're leaving?" Rig asked.

John looked deep into Rig's eyes and could see he was suffering. He glanced down and saw the blood-soaked trousers. "You've been shot."

"Here's what's going to happen," Rig said, stepping towards John. "You're going to sign over every deed you have to James Harris; then you're going to repent for your crimes. Once you're done with that, I'll escort you and your friend to the sheriff, and you'll turn yourself in."

John burst out laughing.

"I'm serious," Rig said.

"Repent? You keep saying that. Who says that?" John asked.

"I don't have much patience left. First start with signing over the deeds, specifically the one to the parcel of land outside town."

"No," John said flatly, knowing Cecil was in the back room and no doubt hearing everything.

Rig raised his hand and pointed it at John. "I'm going to count to ten. When I'm done, you'll be signing the deeds that I see right there on the desk."

"No," John spat.

"One."

"You can count all you want, I'm not doing it," John countered.

"Two."

"Never going to happen," John said.

"Three."

Cecil emerged from the back room and quickly stepped into the office, his pistol out and cocked. "Four."

Rig paused his count and said, "It appears we're in a bit of a standoff."

"Shoot him," John exclaimed.

Cecil pulled the trigger, the hammer fell forward but the pistol didn't fire. He gave the handgun an odd look and cocked it again.

"Shoot him, damn it," John hollered.

Cecil focused his stare on Rig and began to apply pressure to the trigger once more, the hammer dropped but once more the round didn't fire. "What the hell is wrong with this damn thing?" Cecil howled.

"Shoot him, damn you, man, shoot him!" John screamed, his veins throbbing in his neck.

A gunshot cracked, but it wasn't Cecil.

Cecil lowered his pistol, looked at his chest, and touched the exit wound. He held up his bloody hand to his face and said, "I've been shot."

James hobbled into the room and said, "Yes, you have."

Cecil cocked his head and gave James a shocked look before dropping to his knees and falling over dead.

"Where were we?" Rig asked.

James leaned against the wall. He could feel a sense of vertigo setting in.

"How did you know where I was?" Rig asked.

"On account of your fiery red horse hitched outside," James answered.

With few options left, John smiled and said, "I suppose you want me to sign over that land to you."

"Yes, I'd like that," James said.

"I bought it fair and square," John said.

"You bought it with money you stole," Rig declared.

"How about I sign this over to you; then you let me go. I won't bother you again, I swear," John said.

"No, we're taking you to the sheriff. You need to account for what you did tonight," Rig said.

"And what was that?" John asked.

"You attacked an innocent family. You destroyed their house," Rig replied.

"You think I'm going to surrender to you, give you everything I have, then let you turn me over to the sheriff so I can be either hanged or thrown back in jail?" John asked.

"Yes, but I'd also like you to repent as well," Rig said.

John thought for a moment, shook his head, and said, "I'm through with surrendering. No, I won't do anything you ask me to do. If you want these documents, you'll have to take them from me…dead."

James' vision was getting blurry. He could feel the pull of gravity, yet he knew the final clash was about to occur. Knowing that John would draw anyway, James lifted his arm, which felt like a ton of bricks, aimed and fired. The round struck John just below his left clavicle.

John grunted in pain and fell back into the chair behind him. He glanced up at James and started to cough up blood.

James scooted along the wall, closing in on John. Now a few feet from him, James said, "You're an evil man. There is no redemption for someone like you." He cocked the pistol and fired it again at John.

John groaned one last time then died.

"He was going to draw. He was never going to allow us to take him to the sheriff," James said. The vertigo took over and sent him tumbling to the floor.

Rig caught him and placed him in a chair across the desk from John. "You're not looking too good."

James glanced at John and chuckled. "I'm doing better than him."

"That's true," Rig said. "I'm going to go get a doc. You stay put." Rig raced from the office, leaving James.

"I got you," James said to John's lifeless body. "You thought you could come into my town and take everything I worked so hard for. No, no, you were wrong." Looking up to the ceiling, he continued, "Heavenly Father, please forgive me for what I had to do today. I could have turned the other cheek, but doing so would have put my family in jeopardy. I pray you'll forgive me for my actions today, but know that if I have to protect my family, I'd do it all over again." He closed his eyes and blacked out.

CHAPTER THIRTEEN

OCTOBER 5, 1876

MENTRYVILLE, CALIFORNIA

Whuten James opened his eyes, he looked around to find Emma, Scarlet and Christopher standing over him. "Am I dead?"

"On the contrary, you're very much alive," Christopher replied.

Emma went to his side and took his hand. "You've been a sleep for almost two days."

James looked out the window and saw the sun hovering over the mountains to the west. He pulled up the sheet and looked down at his bandaged hip. "How bad was it?"

"Doctor said you probably chipped a bone, and that you lost a lot of blood," Emma answered.

"I last remember being in Mr. Garcia's old office. We had just dealt with John, um, I remember Rig set me in a chair, and then that's it," James said.

"Rig brought the doctor to you, and then they brought you back here. You've been in bed since," Emma said.

"Oh, dear, how's your arm? Are you well?" James asked, touching her hand.

"As Rig said, just a flesh wound," Emma quipped.

James tried to laugh, but he could still feel the weight of fatigue dragging him down. He saw Christopher out of the corner of his eye and asked, "How are you, my good friend?"

"Fine now that I see you're awake. You gave us quite a scare," Christopher said. "I do want to thank you for ridding the town of that scourge."

"It wasn't just me, it was Rig mainly," James said, scooting himself higher in the bed with the help of Emma.

"A lot has happened since you've been napping," Christopher joked.

"Like what?" James asked.

"I've got men already out at the Garcia plot, surveying sites to start drilling—"

Interrupting Christopher, James asked, "So we got the land?"

"We did, but we had to pay for it. I used my money until we get the incorporation back up," Christopher replied.

"Paid for it? Who did we pay?" James asked, his face showing the confusion he was feeling.

"Rig insisted. Since the parcel was acquired by Kemp using ill-gotten money from a bank robbery, Rig had me wire the money via Western Union. It's really a great service," Christopher said, referring to the first wires of money across the nation, which began in 1872.

"That seems fair," James said. He hadn't expected to get the parcel for free but didn't know Rig would be so efficient.

"And you're the owner of the city lots and buildings too. You, my friend, are the largest landowner in Mentryville now," Christopher chirped.

"I am?" James asked. All the shocking news was coming at him fast. "I suppose I'll have to find a way to sell those off or…"

"Or buy them," Emma said with a smile.

"I'm confused. How am I the owner of those city lots?" James asked.

"All I know is your friend handed me a stack of deeds, and they had all been signed over to you from John Kemp," Christopher explained.

What James didn't know was after he'd passed out, Rig had forged the documents to show James was now the rightful owner but had insisted that James pay the bank back since the money used by John had been stolen.

"I suppose I'll buy them," James said, returning Emma's smile. "You were right, a lot has happened. How has the town responded to all of this?"

"Everyone is happy. Though they kept to themselves when John Kemp was here, they now express relief that he and his men were vanquished," Emma replied.

"I'll let you get some more rest. When you're ready to get back to work, your desk is waiting for you, and hopefully we'll have a well in the ground too," Christopher said. He gave everyone in a room a nod and exited.

"And just like that, everything is better than it was before," Emma said.

James thought about her comment and said, "I was going to say it wasn't, because so many horrible things occurred, but in retrospect I can now live my life in full transparency. No more lies, no more secrets. If this has done anything for us as a family, it's made us grow." He paused and a tear came to his eye. "I am sorry that this had to happen at all. I hope you'll forgive me."

Emma squeezed his hand and said, "No more talk of that."

Scarlet hopped on the bed and nestled up next to him. "Don't cry, Papa. We're safe now. Our guardian angel protected us."

James then noticed that Rig wasn't there. "Where is our guardian angel?"

"He left yesterday, said he had to be somewhere. I can only imagine he's off to save someone else," Emma answered.

"Oh no, he's gone? I never got a chance to thank him. He did so much, put his life on the line for us," James said, a deep sadness written on his face.

"I miss him," Scarlet said. "Do you think we'll ever see him again?"

"I don't know, sweetheart, but you can always visit him in your thoughts and prayers," Emma said.

"Maybe we'll cross paths again one day," James said. "Until then let's live our lives in love and gratitude for what he did for us and the town." James pulled Emma and Scarlet close and gave them each a kiss. The heavy weight of dread was lifted, and now he could fulfill his potential and create a lasting legacy for his family. There were many lessons in what had happened, going all the way back to Missouri and the war. No longer would he hide from his sins or keep secrets, for nothing stays hidden forever.

CHAPTER FOURTEEN

OCTOBER 6, 1876

YUMA, ARIZONA TERRITORY

The ride to Yuma took a day longer than it should have, due mainly to Rig's injuries. Several times he contemplated slowing the ride even more than it was, but his determination to see Val pushed him through.

Upon seeing the town in the distance, he picked up his pace, crossed the river via the ferry, and entered town. All seemed the same as it had been when he left, with the streets filled with a mix of civilians and soldiers, all coming and going from saloons and shops. He rode past them all and to the small tent area behind the physical structures east of Main Street. He prayed she'd be there and that she'd kept her word. He had lived long enough to know that some people couldn't be trusted, but something in him said she was the one.

He spotted her tent. A thrill ran through him.

She exited the tent and looked around as if looking for someone. She waved and walked to a man yards away.

Rig pulled back on Fire's reins, coming to a full stop. He watched her interact with the man. She laughed, placed her hand on the man's shoulder, then opened her hand.

The man placed something, what could only have been money, on her palm.

Seeing this, his heart melted. He lowered and shook his head. Glancing back up, he watched her go back into her tent and return with a thick blanket. She handed it to the man, smiled, and waved as the man walked away.

Rig was now confused.

Val smiled broadly, placed her hands on her hips and looked out. She scanned the surroundings, her eyes passing over Rig sitting high in his saddle then coming back to him. Her eyes widened and her mouth opened. "Is that you?" she hollered.

Rig sat tall and prodded Fire to move ahead.

Val ran up to him and took Fire by the bridle. She led Fire to a hitching post and tied him up.

Rig slowly dismounted.

She jumped on him with the excitement of a child, almost knocking him to the ground. "Aren't you a sight for sore eyes!"

He remained quiet.

She kissed him all over his face and said, "I missed you."

Unable to think of anything else, Rig asked, "Who was that man?"

She pulled away from him and gave him a curious look. "What man?"

"The man I just saw give you some money," Rig said,

his tone showing his jealousy.

Her confused look melted away once she realized he was being sensitive about something that really wasn't anything. "I couldn't just sit around twiddling my thumbs, so I decided to make some money sewing."

"You're making money sewing?" Rig asked.

"I know you might be rich and all, but I'm a girl who's had to take care of myself most of my life. I'm still able-bodied, and if I can make a dollar, I will," she said. "Were you jealous?"

"Well, I…"

Smacking him gently on his burly chest, she said, "You were jealous. You thought I'd gone back to my old profession. Well, I can tell you that I'm a woman of my word. We made a deal, and I don't go back on my word."

"I just didn't know what to think," he said.

"Honey, I'm your woman now," she said. "Now come, let's get you cleaned up and put some hot food in your belly." She took his hand and pulled him towards the tent.

He resisted as his leg hurt.

Seeing he was in pain, she asked, "Are you injured?"

"I got a bit hurt, you could say," Rig answered.

"Then let me take care of you," she said sweetly, wrapping her arm around his waist and walking him slowly to the tent.

He stopped her and asked, "You really waited for me?"

Giving him a tender look, she replied, "Of course I did, and you know what, it's not because you gave me the money or that I'd given my word. I did so mainly because I see in you my future. I don't know what it is, but you're a good man, Rig whatever your last name is."

"Buchanan, my last name is Buchanan."

"Rig Buchanan, I waited for you because in you I see a man I can share my life with," Val said.

Never in his life had he ever had anyone talk to him the way she was. "That's the nicest thing anyone has ever said to me."

"I want you to be prepared to hear more words like that 'cause I'm going to keep sayin' them," Val said. "Now let's get you in the tent, undressed, cleaned up, and you can tell me all about your journey."

"Thank you," Rig said.

"For what?"

"For being kind."

She placed her hand on his face and said, "Abundant kindness is missing in this world. It's the one thing that is free yet yields the greatest return."

"Wiser words have never been uttered. Maybe you'll have a future as a writer."

Getting on her toes, she stretched and gave him a kiss on the lips. "Maybe so, I'll think about that later, but right now let's take care of you."

"There's something I should tell you about me," Rig said.

"And what's that?" she asked.

"I have these dreams," he replied.

"What sort of dreams?" she asked giving him a curious stare.

"It's a long story," he said.

"Lucky for you, we have all the time in the world," she said.

The two disappeared into the tent.

THE END

ABOUT THE AUTHOR

G. Michael Hopf is the best-selling author of THE NEW WORLD series and other novels. He spent two decades living a life of adventure before he settled down and became a novelist full time. He is a combat veteran of the United States Marine Corps and a former executive protection agent. He lives with his family in San Diego, CA

Please feel free to contact him at geoff@gmichaelhopf.com with any questions or comments.

www.gmichaelhopf.com

www.facebook.com/gmichaelhopf

Books by G. MICHAEL HOPF

THE NEW WORLD SERIES
THE END
THE LONG ROAD
SANCTUARY
THE LINE OF DEPARTURE
BLOOD, SWEAT & TEARS
THE RAZOR'S EDGE
THOSE WHO REMAIN

NEW WORLD SERIES SPIN OFFS
NEMESIS: INCEPTION
EXIT

THE WANDERER SERIES
VENGEANCE ROAD
BLOOD GOLD
TORN ALLEGIANCE

THE BOUNTY HUNTER SERIES
LAST RIDE
THE LOST ONES
PRAIRIE JUSTICE

ADDITIONAL APOCALYPTIC BOOKS
HOPE (CO-AUTHORED W/ A. AMERICAN)
DAY OF RECKONING
DETOUR: AN APOCALYPTIC HORROR STORY
DRIVER 8: A POST-APOCALYPTIC NOVEL
THE DEATH TRILOGY (WITH JOHN W. VANCE)

ADDITIONAL WESTERN BOOKS
THE LAWMAN
THE RETRIBUTION OF LEVI BASS

Made in the USA
Columbia, SC
05 August 2019